Alice-Miranda

at Sea

Also by Jacqueline Harvey

Alice-Miranda at School
Alice-Miranda on Vacation
Alice-Miranda Takes the Stage

Alice-Miranda

at Sea

JACQUELINE HARVEY

DELACORTE PRESS

Text copyright © 2011 by Jacqueline Harvey
Jacket art and interior illustrations copyright © 2011 by J. Yi

All rights reserved. Published in the United States by Delacorte Press, an imprint of
Random House Children's Books, a division of Random House LLC,
a Penguin Random House Company, New York.
Originally published in paperback by Random House Australia, a division of the
Random House Group, Sydney, in 2011.

Delacorte Press is a registered trademark and the colophon is a
trademark of Random House LLC.

Visit us on the Web! randomhouse.com/kids

Educators and librarians, for a variety of teaching tools, visit us at
RHTeachersLibrarians.com

Library of Congress Cataloging-in-Publication Data
Harvey, Jacqueline.
Alice-Miranda at sea / Jacqueline Harvey. — First American edition.
pages cm
"Originally published in Australia in paperback by Random House Australia Pty Ltd,
a division of the Random House Group, Sydney, in 2011"—Copyright page.
ISBN 978-0-385-74375-4 (hardback) — ISBN 978-0-375-99127-1 (lib. bdg.) —
ISBN 978-0-385-37018-9 (ebook)
[1. Ocean liners—Fiction. 2. Friendship—Fiction. 3. Mystery and detective stories.]
I. Title.
PZ7.H2674785Alg 2014
[Fic]—dc23
2013030813

Printed in the United States of America

10 9 8 7 6 5 4 3 2 1

First American Edition

For Ian and Sandy

Prologue

Neville Nordstrom stared at the screen. His thick vanilla eyebrows furrowed together like a pair of hairy caterpillars and his nose began to twitch.

"Is it really you?" Neville whispered at the computer. But of course there was no reply. His friend had logged out moments ago, signing off with the usual "so long and happy hunting."

They'd been talking via the secure chat area of the club for only a couple of months. But in that time Neville had come to realize that his friend, wherever he was, was the most passionate collector he'd encountered yet. Smart too.

But perhaps not smart enough. Neville was sure that his new friend was conversing under an assumed name; he'd laughed out loud when he saw it. *F. Scott Fitzgerald.* Wasn't that a famous writer—and a dead one at that?

Then again, Neville hadn't exactly been honest either. He wanted to tell his parents about his hobby, but he knew they wouldn't understand. And it was getting harder to keep up the ruse. He'd overheard his mother talking to his father last week—wondering how on earth Neville's shorts could be getting tighter when he was playing soccer every other day. Neville made a mental note not to eat so many doughnuts while he was hunting.

Then, yesterday, his online friend's disguise had begun to slip. He had said too much, and one by one Neville was joining the dots. Neville was almost certain that he was chatting with someone very important—more important than most people in the world, really. And definitely the one man who could help him to save the species. Now all he had to do was prove it.

Chapter 1

Alice-Miranda Highton-Smith-Kennington-Jones turned toward the driver as the limousine weaved its way through the streets from the airport.

"Excuse me, Mr. Fernandez, are we nearly there?" she asked through the opening that separated the driver from his passengers.

The man smiled to himself and kept his eyes firmly on the road ahead. "Soon, miss. Very soon. In fact, just around this corner you will see the sea."

Alice-Miranda clasped her hands together in delight. She nudged Millie and Jacinta, who were sitting either side of her. Millie was fiddling with her camera and Jacinta was staring wide-eyed out the window.

"Look, over there!" Jacinta pointed at the sparkling harbor spread out in front of them.

Millie looked up and craned her neck to get a better view. "Oh, wow! I have to get a photo of that."

"It's a pity we're leaving straight away," Alice-Miranda told her friends. "Barcelona has some very interesting buildings."

"Well, that sounds boring," Jacinta said, and wrinkled her nose.

"No, not at all. Mummy and Daddy once took me to visit an enormous cathedral called the Sagrada Família. It sort of looks like it was made by a giant out of Play-Doh and soft cheese," Alice-Miranda replied.

Hugh Kennington-Jones glanced up from his newspaper. "Not everyone's cup of tea. But Mr. Gaudí's constructions are certainly, um, unique."

"Sounds weird." Jacinta's eyes were fixed on the coastline. "Look! There's a ship. I wonder if that's the *Octavia*."

Cecelia Highton-Smith turned to look out the window. "Oh yes, I think it could be. Aunty Gee is so kind allowing Charlotte and Lawrence to have their wedding on board. It's very clever of them to get married at sea."

Millie lowered the window and snapped away with her camera as the limousine headed toward the dock.

"And hopefully, since we've come all the way to Spain, we might be able to shake off those jolly pesky photographers who don't seem to leave Lawrence and Charlotte alone at the moment." Hugh frowned.

"They're called paparazzi, Daddy, and they're only doing their job," Alice-Miranda informed him.

"Well, it's a stupid job." Millie laid her camera back in her lap. "I really don't understand why people would want to see photographs of Lawrence eating a banana or getting his morning coffee or buying groceries—I mean, he is handsome and everything, but that's just ridiculous."

"Aunt Charlotte will have to get used to it too, I suppose." Alice-Miranda nodded.

"My mother loves them," Jacinta said.

"Who?" Millie asked.

"The paparazzi, of course," Jacinta replied.

Jacinta's mother, Ambrosia Headlington-Bear, spent her life traveling the world looking glamorous, with a trail of hangers-on longer than most red carpets. The last time she had seen her daughter was over ten months ago and their most recent conversation had consisted of a terse exchange about the school play.

The limousine suddenly seemed very small—as though an elephant had hopped on board and no one was willing to acknowledge its presence. Cecelia pursed her lips and wondered if her decision had been the right one.

Millie hastily changed the subject. "I can't believe that we're going on Queen Georgiana's ship. And do you remember when I first met her; I thought she was Mrs. Oliver's sister. She must think I'm completely thick."

"Of course not." Cecelia laughed. "Aunty Gee would have taken it as a compliment. She adores Mrs. Oliver. And there is more than a passing resemblance—everyone says so."

The car rolled to a halt at a set of security gates, where Mr. Fernandez hopped out of the driver's seat to open the trunk for inspection. Hugh lowered the darkly tinted windows and handed over a wad of passports to a young Spanish policeman, who looked in at the group.

"*Hola.*" Alice-Miranda waved. The man grinned. He disappeared into the small sentry building and returned a few minutes later.

"Enjoy your *vacaciones*," the policeman called as he handed the passports back through the window to Alice-Miranda's father.

The car proceeded past the checkpoint toward the ship moored at the end of the dock. No one inside the vehicle noticed the fair-haired boy, with a backpack slung over his right shoulder and a worn leather trumpet case clutched in his left hand, approach the security checkpoint behind them. The lad put his bags down and reached inside his jacket pocket. His outstretched hand trembled as he gave his passport to the dark-eyed officer.

"Billete?"

Neville chewed nervously at his left thumbnail. He wished he'd paid more attention in class since moving to Barcelona. His Spanish was terrible.

"S-s-sorry?" Neville squeaked.

"Your ticket, young man," said the officer, this time in English. "Where are you going?"

"Oh." Neville fumbled around in his jacket pocket and produced another official-looking document.

The officer smiled. "Your bags?"

Neville's stomach flipped. Why did they want his bags? Beads of perspiration formed along his brow.

The officer reached out and was just about to pick up Neville's case when a police motorcycle, siren blaring, turned onto the road. Behind it Neville could see a motorcade of at least six vehicles, adorned with flags on either side of the hoods and speeding toward the checkpoint.

"Antonio, *rápidamente!*" another man called from inside the security booth.

The officer handed Neville his passport and ticket and gestured for him to move on.

"*¡Vete! ¡Vete!*" he ordered, flicking his hand. "Go!"

"Which ship?" Neville wheezed. But the policeman had already turned to greet the incoming fleet.

Neville had no idea who was in that motorcade, but clearly they were much more important than a nervous kid with a battered trumpet case and a ticket to New York.

Chapter 2

"Isn't the ship beautiful?" Alice-Miranda exclaimed as the group stood on the dock beside the gleaming white liner. Snatches of jazz drifted on the air, coming from a small musical ensemble on the open deck above.

"I'll say," Jacinta agreed. "Have you been on her before?"

"No, this is a first for me too. Mummy and Daddy have been quite a few times, but I think they were all 'no children' affairs," Alice-Miranda replied.

"The place is probably packed to the gills with priceless antiques—I can imagine why your Aunty

Gee wouldn't want little monsters running amok," Millie commented.

"And her son, Freddy, has plenty of those," Hugh whispered conspiratorially to Cecelia.

His wife rolled her eyes. Queen Georgiana's seven grandchildren had quite the reputation for their wild behavior—and hence were never at the top of anyone's invitation list, particularly the Queen's own.

"How many people are coming to the wedding?" Millie asked.

"I think at last count there were two hundred eighty-five," said Cecelia. "Charlotte and Lawrie were keen just to have family and close friends."

"I still can't believe *we* got invited," said Millie, nodding toward Jacinta.

"Darling, you and Jacinta *are* like family. Hugh and I have become very fond of you both. And it's lovely for Alice-Miranda to have you here too." Cecelia smiled.

Along the dock black limousines were lined up nose to tail, like ponies on a carousel. Alice-Miranda waved feverishly at Granny Bert and Daisy, who had just arrived with Mrs. Oliver and Mrs. Shillingsworth a couple of cars ahead. The whole Highton-Smith-Kennington-Jones household had been invited to the wedding.

Alice-Miranda waved at an elderly lady wearing a ruby-colored suit. "Hello, Granny," she called. The woman was busily directing a chauffeur who was wrestling with a mountain of luggage. Granny Valentina Highton-Smith, on seeing her only grandchild, called back, "See you on board, darling," and blew her a kiss, which Alice-Miranda promptly reached out and caught and blew straight back again.

"Look, there's Lord Robert and dear cousin Lady Sarah and their gorgeous girls, Poppy and Annie." Cecelia waved furiously at a blond woman wearing a very stylish pink hat and an armful of gold bracelets. A pair of enormous diamonds like two Christmas tree baubles adorned her ears.

"I haven't seen Poppy and Annie for ages." Alice-Miranda waved toward the group. "Well, not since last Christmas at Granny's."

"Another Poppy! So there'll be two Poppys on the ship. That's so confusing," Jacinta said. "We'll have to think what to call them. What's your cousin's surname?"

"Adams," Alice-Miranda replied.

"So we'll have Poppy Adams and Poppy Bauer. We could just call them Poppy A and Poppy B," Jacinta declared.

"Oh dear," Cecelia began. "I'm sorry, girls, but Lily

called a little while ago to say that they aren't going to make it. Granny Bauer is still unwell and needs them to stay on with her for longer."

Heinrich Bauer ran the farm at Highton Hall. His wife, Lily, often helped Cecelia, and Jasper and Poppy were two of Alice-Miranda's closest companions.

"That's bad news," Alice-Miranda replied. "I hope Granny Bauer gets better soon. The wedding just won't be the same without Poppy and Jasper, but at least Millie can take loads of photographs for us to show them when we're home again."

"That sounds perfect, but come along, girls. We want to get settled as quickly as possible." Hugh began to guide the children toward the ship. "There's plenty of time to see everyone when we're on board."

A short line of crewmen, splendidly dressed in dazzling white uniforms, stood on either side of the gangplank. Not that "plank" was the right word at all for the ornate navy-blue bridge and stretch of red carpet that spanned the void between the dock and the ship.

Alice-Miranda insisted on greeting every single one of the crew individually.

"Hello, my name is Alice-Miranda Highton-Smith-Kennington-Jones." She held out her tiny hand. "And

I'm very pleased to meet you. This is my mummy, Cecelia, and my daddy, Hugh, and these are my two friends Millie and Jacinta."

The first sailor gave a small nod and reluctantly took her hand in his.

"Um, nice to meet you, miss. Sir, ma'am." He looked at Mr. Kennington-Jones for approval. Hugh smiled broadly and shook his head in the direction of his effusive daughter.

The exchange was repeated again and again until Alice-Miranda had shaken hands with all of the assembled staff, whose grins widened as she moved from one to the other. She proceeded to skip up the gangplank, where she was greeted by the admiral, a stocky, gray-bearded septuagenarian named Teddy Harding.

"Good morning, miss." He knelt down to greet Alice-Miranda, who promptly introduced herself in the usual way. Admiral Harding looked up to see Cecelia and Hugh arriving behind her. He motioned to the two crewmen on either side to assist him back to his feet.

"Admiral Harding." Cecelia greeted the old man with a kiss on each cheek. "It's wonderful to see you again."

"You're looking as lovely as ever, Cecelia, my dear."
Admiral Harding held Cecelia's hands and took a
step backward.

"And you're the same charming old fox I remember." Hugh raised an eyebrow as the two men shook
hands vigorously.

"Well, I see your little daughter is every bit as gorgeous as her mother." Admiral Harding winked at
Alice-Miranda, who winked right back. "And who do
we have here?" he asked, spying Jacinta and Millie
over Alice-Miranda's shoulder.

"May I introduce you to my good friends from
school, Jacinta Headlington-Bear and Millicent
Jane McLoughlin-McTavish-McNoughton-McGill—
but she likes to be called Millie." Alice-Miranda motioned for them to come forward.

Admiral Harding shook the girls' hands and said
that he was very pleased to meet them. "In fact,
didn't I just meet your parents a little while ago,
Miss Millicent?" he asked, looking perplexed.

From behind the girls, Cecelia raised her finger to
her lips and gently shook her head. She had been
hoping to keep the arrival of Millie's and Jacinta's
parents a surprise until the girls boarded.

"No, I must be mistaken. Probably another couple

on board with the very same name. Imagine that."
Admiral Harding chuckled.

Millie and Jacinta exchanged glances, wondering
what on earth he was talking about.

A tall man in a crisp uniform slid into position beside the admiral, who glowered at his late arrival.

"May I introduce you to our principal medical officer, Dr. Nicholas Lush." Admiral Harding nodded
at the man. "Pity he's yet to find a watch that keeps
good time."

Dr. Lush gulped and his bald head turned the color
of ripe raspberries. "Hello, I'm so very pleased to
meet you," he gushed at Cecelia and Hugh.

"What a delicious name you have, Dr. Lush." Alice-
Miranda stretched forward to shake his hand. He
hesitated a moment, then reached out and took her
hand in his. "It's very nice to meet you, sir."

"Mmm, yes," Nicholas mumbled.

"But I hope we don't see you again," Jacinta said.

Dr. Lush looked at Jacinta as though he was in-
specting a nasty fungal infection.

"Jacinta—rude!" Millie whispered behind her left
hand, before promptly elbowing her friend in the
ribs with her right arm.

"I didn't mean it like that. I'm sure you're a perfectly

nice person, Dr. Lush, it's just that if we see you it means we're sick, and I don't plan on being sick for one second," Jacinta finished. The group looked at her and laughed.

Dr. Lush sneered. He rather hoped he didn't see the little brats again either. He hadn't counted on there being any children on board. In his experience, particularly with Her Majesty's own grandchildren, they only created problems and a lot more work.

Admiral Harding signaled to three young stewards standing to his left.

"Well, these lads will show you to your quarters. We're departing at two p.m. I hope you'll join us on deck for a good old-fashioned send-off."

Chapter 3

Meanwhile, out on the dock, guests were scattering this way and that as the flag-flying motorcade pulled up beside the gangplank. Aunty Gee had delayed their arrival by several minutes as she stopped to talk with the handsome, dark-eyed policeman at the security checkpoint. He rather reminded her of her late husband, Leopold.

In an operation requiring military precision, Queen Georgiana and her household were to be on board the ship and ensconced in their suites within the next twenty minutes. However, the royal standard was not yet flying and protocol demanded that the Queen not board the ship until the flag was in place.

"Dalton, whatever is the delay?" Aunty Gee enquired of her personal bodyguard.

Dalton pushed his earpiece harder into his ear. "I'm not entirely sure, ma'am, but I think someone has . . . um . . . misplaced the flag," he replied sheepishly.

"Well, tell them to hurry up and find it. I've had two glasses of water on the way from the airport, and whilst *I* have an impeccable constitution, it would seem that my aged bladder does not," the Queen ordered.

Aunty Gee scanned the quayside, and soon her eyes fell upon just what she was looking for.

"Dalton, Mrs. Marmalade, why don't you hop out and see about this silly holdup?" she commanded. With both her bodyguard and lady-in-waiting out of the car, Aunty Gee waited a moment before alighting from the vehicle on the far side. Fortunately her entire entourage seemed to be gazing at the empty flagpole, as if by mere power of mutual thought they could zip the flag into place. With some urgency, Aunty Gee fled to the public convenience located opposite the ship and was out again before anyone had time to miss her.

On her return to the vehicle she spotted a fair-haired lad staring up at the *Octavia*.

"Are you joining us?" Aunty Gee asked the boy and motioned toward the case he was hiding behind his left leg.

Neville moved his head ever so slightly and wondered why the woman speaking to him seemed vaguely familiar. He had been up and down the quayside five times now and still hadn't been able to work out which ship was heading where. His mission was made doubly difficult by several large containers lining the dock obscuring some of the ships' names.

"A-A-America?" he squeaked in an octave befitting a chorister.

"What was that, dear? A miracle?" Aunty Gee repeated, staring at the boy and wondering at the cause of his unusually high voice. "Yes, it will be a miracle if we ever board this ship today. Well, you'd better get a move on. They'll want you on there before they'll let me up. And where are your parents?"

Neville gulped. If he said that he was traveling on his own, surely she'd call security. He was thinking about running when he looked across and saw her. A miracle indeed.

He pointed to the bottom of the gangplank, where a woman wearing a huge black hat and oversized sunglasses was teetering toward the ship.

{19}

"Is that your mother?" Aunty Gee asked.

Neville managed a small nod.

"Well, hurry up and join her, then." Aunty Gee turned and called to the woman, "Dear! Excuse me, dear, you've left your son behind."

The woman did not turn around at all. "Run along there, lad. Obviously your mother has a hearing problem," Aunty Gee tutted as she dived back into her own car and waited.

Neville Nordstrom was on his way up the gangplank before he had time to think. He reached the woman with the umbrella-sized hat and stood rigid behind her, like a stalk on a mushroom. No one seemed to notice him at all.

Well aware that Her Majesty was waiting to board, Admiral Harding was keeping his greetings to a bare minimum. A swift shake of the hand or nod of the head was all the time he could afford. When Ambrosia Headlington-Bear reached the head of the queue she pulled the earphones from her ears in anticipation of a lengthy welcome speech. She'd been looking forward to this moment. It wasn't every day one boarded the *Octavia* as a guest of the Queen.

At the same moment, First Officer Whitley Prendergast appeared and whispered to a much-relieved Admiral Harding that they had located the missing flag, which was now on its way to the flagpole. He didn't mention that it had been found hidden in one of the stewards' lockers. How it got there was a mystery indeed.

Ambrosia tapped her Prada heels, removed her sunglasses and stared at the admiral.

"Yes, welcome. Mr. and Mrs. Headlington-Bear, I presume?" Admiral Harding greeted her. He made a point of researching his passengers well and prided himself on knowing many on sight. "I'm sorry to rush you along there, ma'am, but we have to keep moving. Don't want to be late, now."

"Yes, but he's . . . ," Ambrosia began.

"Yes, it's lovely to have you on board," Admiral Harding steamrolled as the young purser beside him checked off the list of names. "Hurry along, please, ma'am. We're running a wee bit late."

Several guests were now pushing up behind. The admiral checked his watch. It was 1:45 p.m. How they would have Queen Georgiana installed in her suite by two p.m. was anyone's guess, but if the lines of perspiration trailing down the side of his face were any indication, Admiral Harding would do it or, at the very least, die trying.

In one swift move, Neville's hand flew out from behind Ambrosia, holding aloft his passport and ticket for anyone who cared to see.

But nobody noticed, and Neville found himself swept along in the woman's wake. His heart hammered inside his chest as he reached into his jacket pocket for his inhaler.

As they passed by what looked to be a dining room, Neville felt rather glad he hadn't bothered to upgrade his ticket. Discount economy passage to the USA looked much better than he had imagined.

Chapter 4

"**Y**our room, ma'am." A young steward held open the door to Ambrosia's suite.

"But it's belowdecks," she whined. "We'll see about that." The steward caught sight of Neville, who was now stranded in the middle of the hallway. "Are you all right there, son?"

Neville nodded.

"Where are my bags?" Ambrosia called from inside her room. "I need to get changed. Now!"

The freckle-faced crewman sighed, then disappeared into the suite. He was glad he hadn't been allocated to look after this woman for the whole voyage and felt very sorry for the steward who had.

Neville dived toward a door opposite, turned the handle and, to his great relief, found it unlocked. He slipped inside, shut the door behind him and exhaled deeply. He had no idea if this was his room, but he imagined someone would tell him soon enough.

He put his backpack on the floor but kept hold of the case. A small entrance hall led through to a sitting room with a comfy-looking sofa, a walnut writing desk and a long glass-fronted bookcase loaded with leather-bound volumes. A small dining table for two stood at the far end. The suite seemed quite large, really. Much like his nan's front room, he thought, but a bit posher.

There was another door at the end of the room, which Neville supposed would lead to the bedroom. After a minute's hesitation, his curiosity got the better of him and he crept toward the closed door, listened for a moment, then turned the polished brass handle.

Finding the room empty, Neville took a moment to look around. It had a huge bed in the center with a built-in mahogany headboard and another comfortable-looking couch in the corner. A row of wardrobes took up one wall, and three portholes, like giant fish eyes, blinked at him from another. Another door revealed a marble bathroom complete with shower, toilet, vanity and an impressively large bath.

Neville really hoped this room *was* his. He could be quite comfortable here for the next eight days.

He sat down on the couch beside the bed and finally let go of the case, placing it on the floor in front of him. Neville began to think. But after a minute he realized that was a mistake. Thinking didn't help at all. His mother would be worried sick, and his father, well, it didn't even bear considering what he would do when he found out.

Instead he decided to focus on the mission ahead. "Positive self-talk, Neville, that's what you need," he whispered to himself. When he'd suggested to his Internet friend that perhaps he could help Neville with his project, there seemed a longer-than-usual delay in his response. As his friend was normally a big talker, Neville wondered if there was a problem. He decided to tell his friend that he'd worked out who he was. That was a big mistake—all contact had ceased immediately. Neville wondered if it had something to do with his public image. Maybe there was a reason why his friend didn't want to tell everyone about his hobby. But Neville didn't intend to tell anyone else. He just needed some help, and this was the one person who could give it to him.

And then the other morning, as Neville was riding the bus to school, he came face to face with the answer to his problem. A billboard showing a ship leaving Barcelona Port, with the Statue of Liberty superimposed in the background. That was it! He would go in person, and then surely he couldn't be ignored. It was something his dad had always said: "You've got to meet people. Turn up and they can't give you the brush-off so easily."

Neville bought his ticket online using the two hundred euros his nan had sent him for his birthday and Christmas. Luckily he kept his money in the bank and his parents trusted him to have his own access card. Then he'd shaken his savings from his piggy bank. He told his parents he was staying with a friend, Romeo, and that they were spending a long weekend at soccer camp.

He'd even printed the permission note himself. It was lucky his mother's Spanish was even worse than his, as Neville had copied the text straight from an article on the Internet about a pet show.

"When are we going to meet this Romeo?" Neville's mother had asked as he grabbed his sports bag and headed out the door. His trumpet case was safely stowed in the back of the shed. He'd pick it up on the way.

"Soon, Mum," Neville mumbled. He didn't want to disappoint her.

But Neville's mother was so grateful that her son had found a friend and joined a sports team, she wasn't concerned at all. She loved their new life in Spain. For her it was all about the beach and golf and friends at the country club just down the road from their villa. As long as her son was happy, she was happy too. Her husband's earth-moving business was doing exceedingly well. It seemed as if half of Spain was being developed into villas for cashed-up retirees, and bulldozers were in big demand. And ever since they'd met that charming Smedley Sykes, their lives had taken a sharp turn for the better.

Neville realized when he booked his passage that he'd be away for more than just the weekend. The ship would take eight days to reach New York, and then he would have to find his way south to his ultimate destination. He'd heard that Americans were very friendly, so he was hoping to get a lift to save money. Neville wished he could have flown, but the cheapest fare was five times what he had saved up. He'd explained everything in a letter to his parents, which he posted on the way to the dock. They'd receive it early the following week, and he hoped that at least then they wouldn't worry too much. Neville could do all the worrying for them—especially about what his father would say to him when he finally arrived home.

And now here he was. Almost on his way. Neville decided to stay put for now. He hadn't realized just how tired he was until he sat down. His eyelids felt like lead and he was struggling to stay awake. A minute later Neville's head fell backward and he was fast asleep.

Chapter 5

Alice-Miranda, Millie and Jacinta were sharing a suite next door to Hugh and Cecelia. Three single beds had been installed so the girls could bunk in together.

"Why don't you have a look around and get settled and we'll see you back on deck in ten minutes," Cecelia instructed the group. "I hope you like the suite—it was always our favorite when Charlotte and I were young."

"It's gorgeous, Mummy," Alice-Miranda replied, looking around at the expansive sitting room with its antique bookcase, grandfather clock and enormous fireplace. "But I can't imagine we'll be spending much time in here. There'll be far too many other things to do."

Although the room would have been right at home at Highton Hall, there were some touches that set it apart, most particularly the overstuffed cushions embroidered with Queen Georgiana's coat of arms. The bedroom was another thing altogether, with its candy-pink duvets and cabinet full of china dolls.

"We'll see you on the Promenade Deck, darling," Cecelia called, then retreated and left the girls to explore.

"When did your mother unpack our things?" Millie quizzed.

"I don't think she did," said Alice-Miranda. "Unless Mummy has the ability to be in two places at once."

"Maybe Mrs. Shillingsworth did it?" suggested Jacinta.

"No, Mummy and Daddy have given everyone from home strict instructions that they're not to lift a finger at all. The wedding is a holiday."

Not only had the children's clothes been unpacked, the suitcases had been stowed, and even Brummel Bear, Alice-Miranda's well-loved teddy, had found a resting place against the pillow on the middle bed.

A sharp knock on the suite door interrupted the

girls' conversation. Alice-Miranda walked from the bedroom to the hallway off the sitting room, where she was met by a stern-looking gentleman in a starched white uniform who had obviously let himself in.

"Hello." Alice-Miranda smiled. "My name is Alice-Miranda Highton-Smith-Kennington-Jones." She offered her tiny hand.

"Good afternoon, miss," the man replied. "My name is Winterstone, and I have been assigned to look after you for the voyage." His lips twitched as he spoke.

"Well, it's very nice to meet you, Mr. Winterstone," Alice-Miranda replied. "Was it you who unpacked all of our things?"

"Yes, miss. I trust everything is in order." Winterstone walked past her into the sitting room and over to the couch, where he produced from his top pocket a small retractable ruler. He measured upward and down, then repositioned the cushions, just so.

"Please, don't fuss," Alice-Miranda instructed. "We'll try not to make a mess."

"Nothing will give me more pleasure than to spend my time straightening up after you," said Winterstone.

"Really? I can't imagine that it's a pleasure to

straighten up after anyone. And it's rather unfair too." Alice-Miranda frowned. "At school Mrs. Howard is always running around after the girls, but at least this term she's taught everyone to make their own beds. By the end of each day the poor woman is exhausted."

Before Alice-Miranda could finish speaking, the bathroom door slammed shut and loud squeals emanated from within the bedroom.

"I want the bed nearest the window," came Jacinta's voice.

"I saw it first," said Millie. There was a *whump* and a soft crash, then the two girls laughed uproariously. Another loud thud was followed by silence.

"Goodness, are you all right in there?" Alice-Miranda called.

Jacinta emerged first. Her hair was rumpled and she looked as if she'd just fought off a tiger.

"We're fine," she giggled. "We just had a wrestle over the beds. Millie fell off but she's okay."

"Jacinta, this is Mr. Winterstone. He unpacked our things," Alice-Miranda informed her.

Jacinta stared. "Is that your real hair?"

"Jacinta!" Alice-Miranda rebuked. "I'm sorry, Mr. Winterstone, she didn't mean that."

"Yes I did," Jacinta continued. "It must be *so* long on that side." She pointed to his left ear. "Do you have to use product to comb it over and stick it down?"

"Jacinta . . ." Alice-Miranda tried again.

"It's all right, miss," Winterstone began. "I understand that my hair can be a source of fascination for the young and old alike. Yes, it is my own and it's all I have, so unlike others who may be tempted to opt for a less-is-more approach, I'm afraid that I haven't yet been able to bring myself to part with the little I have left."

"I think it's perfectly lovely hair," said Alice-Miranda.

Jacinta crossed her arms in front of her. "Well, no offense, Mr. Winterstone, but I think you'd look much better with a crew cut. My grandfather got one a few years ago and he's never looked back."

"Thank you for your learned opinion, miss."

"Mr. Winterstone, I should have introduced you properly. This is my friend Jacinta."

"Charmed." Winterstone narrowed his steel-gray eyes.

Millie joined the girls in the sitting room.

"And this is Millie," Alice-Miranda finished.

"Hello." Millie smiled sheepishly. "I heard Alice-

Miranda say that you unpacked our bags. Thanks very much for that."

"It was my pleasure," Winterstone replied crisply.

Somehow, Millie didn't really believe him.

"We'd better get moving," Alice-Miranda informed the group. "We have to meet Mummy and Daddy on deck in a minute."

"May I say, Miss Jacinta, that your own hair is looking rather untidy?" Winterstone remarked. "Would you like me to fix it for you?"

Jacinta shook her head. "No, I can do it."

"Before you head off and run riot among the guests, I am obliged to explain a few things to you regarding the voyage, so I would appreciate it if you would take a seat for a moment."

"Oh, I promise, Mr. Winterstone, there'll be no running riot—" Alice-Miranda began.

"Shh." Winterstone raised a bony finger to his lips.

"But what I wanted to say—"

"Might you listen for just a moment, young lady?" Winterstone's stare silenced the tiny child.

Alice-Miranda and Millie sat down on the long couch and Jacinta plonked onto the armchair, throwing the cushion on the floor. Winterstone drew in a sharp breath and made a fist with his left hand. He reached down with his right and picked up the cushion, clutching it against his chest as he spoke.

"Firstly, I may be reached any time of the day or night by pressing number nine on the telephone. You will find one beside the beds, another next to the lounge here and the third in the bathroom beside the lavatory," Winterstone began.

"That won't be necessary. I'm sure we won't be calling you in the middle of the night, Mr. Winterstone," said Alice-Miranda.

"I don't know about that." Jacinta bit back a grin. "What if I'm thirsty?"

"Jacinta." Millie rolled her eyes.

Winterstone exhaled slowly. "As we will be traveling close to the coast, if you would like to send any mail, there will be a tender picking up and delivering post each morning—depending on the weather, of course."

"That's lovely," Alice-Miranda fizzed. "I had hoped I would be able to send Miss Grimm a postcard or two. And I promised Mrs. Smith I would let her know all about the food."

"You're so old-fashioned, Alice-Miranda," snorted Jacinta. "Who sends letters these days?"

"I think letters are lovely. It's so much nicer to get

something in the post. I mean, emails are wonderful, but there's something truly delicious about a letter," said Alice-Miranda.

"On that, miss, I must agree with you." Winterstone nodded.

Jacinta shook her head. "You won't catch me wasting time writing any silly old letters. Boring!"

"If I may continue?" Winterstone interrupted. "There is a small refrigerator located behind this panel." He pulled open the bottom door of the china cabinet, revealing a miniature fridge loaded with juices, bottled water and soft drinks.

"See, Jacinta," Millie piped up. "You won't need to call Mr. Winterstone in the middle of the night. Everything's here already."

"Now, there are three room keys." Winterstone handed the girls one each. "Try not to lose them. Is there anything else you need at this point?"

"No, thank you, Mr. Winterstone, I don't think so. You've been extremely helpful." Alice-Miranda smiled.

"Very good, miss." He gave a small bow, then turned and left the room.

Millie pulled a face. "He's a bit weird, don't you think?"

"I'm sure he's perfectly lovely," Alice-Miranda

countered. "Perhaps he was just a little upset about his hair."

"Well, I'd be upset if I had hair like that too," Jacinta called from the bathroom, where she had gone to rearrange her own messy locks.

"That's not what I meant." Alice-Miranda frowned. "He might have been embarrassed."

"I don't think he likes children very much," Millie went on.

"Why do you think that?" Alice-Miranda asked.

"He's got wobbly eyes," Millie concluded. "And they're the color of wet cement."

"I don't think his eye color suggests a dislike of children," Alice-Miranda replied.

Jacinta emerged from the bathroom looking more her neat and tidy self. "Well, I agree with Millie," she declared.

"Come on," Alice-Miranda urged. "Let's go and see everyone."

Chapter 6

"Good afternoon, Admiral Harding," Queen Georgiana greeted the commander at the top of the gangplank. He was about to speak when the clamor of bagpipes rang out around the ship.

"That will be quite enough of that," Aunty Gee whispered to Dalton, who promptly murmured into his sleeve, silencing the kilt-wearing musician mid-bar.

"Good afternoon, Your Majesty," said Admiral Harding with a slight bow. "It's wonderful to have you aboard."

"It's wonderful to be here finally." Aunty Gee

arched her left eyebrow and glanced toward the flag rippling on the main masthead.

"We're hoping to push off at two, ma'am. All passengers have arrived."

"Marvelous. Let's get everyone up onto the Promenade Deck, throw some streamers and start the party." She smiled.

Admiral Harding nodded.

Aunty Gee glanced at her lady-in-waiting, who looked as if she'd sucked a whole tree's worth of lemons. "Oh, for heaven's sake, Mrs. Marmalade, it's a wedding, woman. A party. I don't know about you, but this week I plan to have a jolly good time—so might I suggest you loosen up a little, dear, and enjoy yourself?"

Dalton barely suppressed a smirk. He wasn't a fan of old Marmalade's. The two had been with Queen Georgiana for many years, and there was no love lost between them. It warmed his heart to hear Her Majesty giving the old girl a stern talking-to. Marmalade, in her aqua twinset and pearls, dropped her eyes to the floor.

"Dalton," Aunty Gee snapped, "while I hope you enjoy yourself too, I suggest you be on your game this week. We can't afford to have any *incidents*."

Dalton gulped, clearly recalling their last outing with the Highton-Smith-Kennington-Joneses, which had almost ended in disaster.

On that occasion, Aunty Gee had been mistaken yet again for Dolly Oliver, this time by crooks intent on stealing Dolly's formula for miraculous, miniaturized frozen food.

"Would you like to go to your suite and freshen up, ma'am?" Admiral Harding glanced at his watch. "We have a few minutes."

"No, I'm quite all right. I think I'd like to head straight up and see everyone. I've been looking forward to this for months."

Dalton was surprised that Her Majesty no longer required a visit to the facilities after she had been giving them all the hurry-up in the car, but he thought it best not to ask.

And with that, Aunty Gee led the way to the Promenade Deck, where she found her goddaughter, Cecelia; her dearest friend in the world, Valentina; and the family she considered as much her own as any other.

The girls left their suite and scurried upstairs to meet Hugh and Cecelia on the Promenade Deck. There were loads of people gathering, most of whom

Alice-Miranda recognized as friends of her parents, or relatives she only ever saw at large celebrations.

"Isn't that . . . ?" Millie squinted into the light. "That's my mother over there!" She ran toward a flame-haired woman standing beside Mrs. Oliver on the open deck. "Mummy, what are you doing here?"

Pippa McNoughton-McGill turned and hugged her daughter into her outstretched arms. "Hello, Mill. Didn't think we were going to let you have all the fun, did you, sweetheart?"

"Now, who's this gorgeous girl?" Hamish McLoughlin-McTavish appeared next to his wife and tapped Millie on the shoulder.

"Dad! This is the best surprise ever!" Millie squealed. "I can't believe you kept it a secret—we only saw you a couple of weeks ago at the play and you didn't mention anything!"

Ambrose McLoughlin-McTavish walked up behind his granddaughter and put his hands over her eyes. "Wonderful occasion, isn't it?"

"Grandpa!" Millie wriggled free. "You're here too?"

"He's with me, dear," said Mrs. Oliver. During the last term break Dolly Oliver had been reunited with her old friend Ambrose McLoughlin-McTavish when Millie had gone to stay with Alice-Miranda. Now both widowed, Mrs. Oliver and Ambrose were rather enjoying each other's company.

Alice-Miranda and Jacinta joined Millie's family reunion.

"Hello there, young lady." Pippa leaned down and kissed Alice-Miranda's cheek. "And, Jacinta, it's lovely to see you again too," she said, and gave her a hug.

Cecelia Highton-Smith approached the group. "I see you've found your surprise, Millie."

"You're so sneaky," Millie admonished. "But in the nicest possible way, of course."

"Well, Charlotte and Lawrence insisted we invite your parents. As it turns out, Cha and Pippa knew each other a little bit at school—I'm much older, so we didn't meet back then. And would you believe that Lawrence and Hamish were only a couple of years apart at Fayle too?" Cecelia scanned the gathering crowd as they began to line the side of the deck.

Jacinta fiddled with a strand of hair. Cecelia glanced over at her, then searched the sea of faces.

"It's all right, Cee," Jacinta whispered. "You don't have to let me down gently. I know my parents have far more important things to do."

"No, that's not the case at all," Cecelia reassured her. "Your parents are definitely on board. I checked with the first officer and he said that they arrived just before Aunty Gee."

Jacinta looked as though she'd swallowed a fly. "Really? My mother and father are here? On board the *Octavia*?"

"Yes, darling." Cecelia stroked the top of Jacinta's head.

"Isn't that fantastic?" Alice-Miranda was wide-eyed. "I've wanted to meet your parents forever, and now we get to spend five whole days with them. Shall we go and find them?"

At that moment, a blast of trumpets heralded the arrival of the official party.

"My lords, ladies and gentlemen, I present Her Majesty, Queen Georgiana," a uniformed page announced with great vigor.

Aunty Gee, accompanied by the admiral, stepped onto a small raised platform in the middle of the crowd, to the delight of everyone on board.

"And now," Aunty Gee announced, "please join me in welcoming our guests of honor and the real reason we have all gathered together for this wonderful time of celebration. I give to you one of my beloved goddaughters, Miss Charlotte Highton-Smith, and her fiancé, Mr. Lawrence Ridley." Aunty Gee could not have looked prouder.

The group clapped and cheered, and there was even a wolf whistle or two coming from the end of the promenade.

"Manners!" Granny Bert, the Highton-Smith-Kennington-Joneses' retired housekeeper, tutted at Max, their stable hand, when she caught him removing his fingers from his mouth.

Charlotte looked stunning in a white pantsuit with navy trim and a matching hat, her arm linked through Lawrence's. He looked equally stylish in a navy sports jacket and white trousers. His jet-black hair glistened in the sun, and his ebony eyes gazed adoringly at his wife-to-be. When he smiled his movie-star smile, almost every woman on the ship went weak at the knees.

"Gosh, he's gorgeous!" Jacinta swooned.

Millie and Alice-Miranda exchanged glances and giggled. Millie began to snap away, taking photographs of Charlotte and Lawrence and the rest of the guests.

Alice-Miranda raced over to greet her aunt. Charlotte scooped the girl into her arms and peppered her face with kisses.

"This is the best day ever!" Alice-Miranda exclaimed. "Well, except for Wednesday, when you get married." She leaned across to kiss Lawrence's cheek.

"You are a funny thing." Charlotte beamed.

"And where's that son of mine?" Lawrence glanced around looking for Lucas.

"There he is, with Sep." Alice-Miranda wriggled out of Charlotte's arms and ran to greet her soon-to-be cousin.

"Hello!" she cried above the ship's horn, which had begun to blast. "Lucas!" She tapped him on the shoulder.

The dark-haired boy turned and smiled at Alice-Miranda.

"Isn't this fun?" she exclaimed.

"Like a fairy tale." He shook his head. "I can't believe we're here on Queen Georgiana's ship. If you'd have told me this would be my life six months ago, I'd have said you were crazy."

It was true; a lot of things had changed in a short time for Lucas Nixon. Until recently, Lucas hadn't known his father's name, let alone that he was one of the world's most sought-after film stars. When Lucas had first met Alice-Miranda and Jacinta on a recent school holiday, he had been more than a little angry and confused. He had been expelled from school, in

{45}

what was a most unfortunate mistake, and sent to stay with his aunt Lily, uncle Heinrich and cousins Jasper and Poppy at their farmhouse on the grounds of Highton Hall. To make matters worse, Lucas had felt completely abandoned by his mother when she had gone away to work in the United States.

But after a couple of weeks, the mystery of his true identity began to unravel, and now life as he knew it would never be the same. Lucas had just spent his first term at Fayle School for Boys on the other side of the village from Winchesterfield-Downsfordvale Academy for Proper Young Ladies, the school Alice-Miranda, Millie and Jacinta attended. Fayle was fantastic, as far as Lucas was concerned, and within a very short time he felt as if he'd been there forever. His new best friend and roommate, Septimus Sykes, had arrived just before him, and the two lads had quickly become as close as any brothers. Lucas could hardly believe how good life was.

Septimus Sykes was a lovely lad, with a rather unfortunate immediate family. His sister, Sloane, had for a brief period been Jacinta's roommate at Winchesterfield-Downsfordvale, until she was caught up in some very nasty business with her mother, September. Septimus had steadfastly refused to leave school, where for the first time in his life he felt he truly belonged. His sister and mother, on the other hand, had departed the village in such a rush there were still tire marks in the school driveway. They'd fled to Spain, where Sep's father, Smedley, who knew nothing of what had gone on, was doing very well with his new property developing business. Apparently the Sykeses were very happy with their new life in the sun.

Millie and Jacinta joined Lucas, Sep and Alice-Miranda as the ship lurched away from the dock. Aunty Gee, to the horror of Mrs. Marmalade, was busy distributing streamers from her apparently bottomless handbag. Family and friends waved at the dockhands down below as shouts of "goodbye and farewell" were carried away on the breeze.

Belowdecks, Neville Nordstrom was jolted awake by the blasting ship's horn. Groggy and somewhat confused, Neville took a moment to remember where he was. At least the ship was moving, he thought.

In the suite opposite, Ambrosia Headlington-Bear was having a terrible time deciding what to wear. She had come aboard in black but feared that was far too French for a Spanish send-off. Three multicolored outfits lay across the bed. She really didn't know what to do. Without Henri, her stylist, getting dressed was rather more difficult than she remembered.

Chapter 7

"I can't believe your brother was invited to that wedding without us," September Sykes whined as she sat up to rub suntan lotion on her overcooked shoulders. "And he wouldn't even tell me where they were going. Said something about it being a secret to make sure that it was all private. Who wants to have a private wedding, anyway? I'd have sold the whole thing to *Gloss and Goss* magazine to pay for the honeymoon. Sloane? Are you even listening to me, Sloane?" September growled as she glanced over at her daughter.

Sloane, lying meters away on a matching sun lounge, rolled away from her mother and turned the music in her ears up louder. An unopened letter fell out of the magazine she was thumbing through. Addressed to "Miss Sloane Sykes, Villa Del Mar, Castelldefels, Spain," the envelope, just like the two she'd received earlier in the month, felt like silk.

Typical, Sloane had thought. She probably has her own silkworm factory just to provide her stationery.

Sloane had been more than a little surprised to receive the first letter. It had sat under the jewelry box on her dressing table for a full week before she decided to open it. And when she did, it wasn't at all what she had imagined. But then again, Alice-Miranda Highton-Smith-Kennington-Jones was hardly normal, now, was she? Instead of the sound telling-off Sloane had expected, Alice-Miranda had prattled on about what a pity it was that she had left school and how she was sure they could have worked things out with Miss Grimm and it really wasn't Sloane's fault and probably there were lots of circumstances that had contributed to her mother's actions because grown-ups are so very complicated.

Sloane was sorely tempted to tear it up right then and there, but something made her stop. Instead she put the letter in her top dresser drawer and wondered if she would hear from her again. And like clockwork, the following week another letter arrived. This one described the end-of-term activities and how well Sep was doing and said it was so lovely for Lucas to have such a good friend, seeing that he'd had rather a rough trot the past few years. Alice-Miranda asked how Sloane was settling into her new school and if she was enjoying her life in the sun.

Sloane's nosy mother had missed seeing the first letter. Her father had picked up the mail that day, which was just as well. Sloane didn't feel like being subjected to the Spanish Inquisition from her mother about why the little princess was writing to her. She'd successfully intercepted the second letter, and now there was a third. Sloane slid off the sun lounge and sloped off into the garden.

"Where are you going, Sloane?" September demanded. "Can you pop inside and get Mummy some corn chips and dip? I'm a bit peckish."

Sloane ignored her mother and headed to the front steps of the villa. She would be safe there, seeing as just after they moved in, September had seen a giant skink and run off screaming to the back of the house. Sloane told her mother that Spanish skinks were deadly (which of course they're not) and that they only lived out the front of the house, closest to the ocean. Her mother now steadfastly refused to go anywhere near the beach and spent her days reclining by the pool out the back.

"So what news do you have for me this time, little girl?" Sloane murmured while she slid her finger under the flap of the envelope. She then read the letter aloud.

Dear Sloane,

I hope that you are very well and enjoying life in Spain. It's the final week of term and Miss Grimm has arranged a whole school working bee at Miss Hephzibah's. The boys at Fayle are joining us, and afterward there is a huge picnic planned. As you can imagine, Mrs. Smith has been cooking nonstop. She told me she's making apple tarts and strawberry sponge cake and chocolate torte, and that was just for starters.

Sloane's stomach grumbled. If there was one thing she did miss about her old school, it was the delicious morning and afternoon teas.

Miss Hephzibah's house is coming along beautifully too. Daddy sent our builders over and they've already fixed the roof, and I know Miss Hephzibah and your granny, Henrietta, have been making plans to turn part of the house into a training college for teachers. Miss Grimm and Professor Winterbottom are busy working out the curriculum and having interviews for new staff. And I can't wait until the end of the week, because we're being whisked off to a secret location for Aunt Charlotte and Uncle Lawrence's wedding. Sep is coming too, but I suppose you knew that already because Mummy would have had to check with your mother and father about him going. I've been asked to be a flower girl, which is terribly exciting. My dress is the most gorgeous shell-pink. I promise to send some photographs. If you have a spare minute I would love to hear your news.

With all best wishes,
Alice-Miranda

Sloane tucked the letter back into the envelope.

"As if I'd want to see your stupid photographs." She rolled her eyes. "And don't expect to get any news from me anytime soon, you little twit."

But reading the letter gave Sloane a niggly twinge in her stomach. Her new school, though well-equipped, was not the same as Winchesterfield-Downsfordvale, with its amazing facilities and clever teachers. She had no ear for languages, and truth be told, Sloane was finding it awfully hard to make any friends.

Her thoughts were interrupted by an ear-piercing scream coming from the rear of the villa.

"Help! Heeeeelp!" September shrieked.

Sloane arrived to find her mother standing on her sun lounge, squealing like a stuck pig.

"What's the matter, Mother?" Sloane asked.

"There ... down there ... it's a ... a ... skink!" September held her hands over her eyes and shuddered.

"Really? A skink?" Sloane inquired, looking completely nonplussed.

"You know they're deadly, Sloane. If Mummy gets bitten, well, that's it." September had now begun to cry.

Sloane couldn't help enjoying the scene in front of her. And she wasn't keen to tell her mother the truth about the not-so-deadly Spanish skinks either.

"I'll get it," Sloane offered.

"Oh, darling, be careful. I don't know what I'd do if ..." Her mother's voice trailed away.

Sloane grabbed her towel from the recliner next to her mother's and threw it over the unsuspecting reptile. She scooped the wriggling lizard into a ball and promptly walked around to the front of the villa, where she released the frightened beast into the grass.

"Off you go." Sloane gave him a grin as he shot off under the villa. "I know, she's terrifying."

Poolside, September Sykes checked carefully before she climbed down from the safety of her sun lounge. She raced across the hot tiles into the kitchen, slamming the terrace door behind her.

"Well, that's no use." She opened the pantry and pulled out a giant box of corn chips. "How am I supposed to get my tan now?"

Chapter 8

B ack on the *Octavia,* family and friends were catching up, nattering about this and that. There was still no sign of Jacinta's parents so Alice-Miranda asked her mother if it was all right for her and the other children to explore the ship. Hopefully they would come across them during their sight-seeing.

"You'll have to check with Aunty Gee, darling," Cecelia replied. "It's her ship, after all, and some places might be off-limits."

Alice-Miranda found Aunty Gee chatting with her granny, Valentina Highton-Smith.

"Hello, Aunty Gee. Hello, Granny." She executed a perfect curtsy.

"There you are, darling girl," Granny Valentina replied. "How are you enjoying the ship?"

"It's wonderful!" Alice-Miranda beamed. "Aunty Gee, I've come to ask you a question."

"Yes, what is it, dear?" The older woman leaned forward. Tiny flecks of powder sat in the smile lines that had taken up permanent residence on Aunty Gee's face.

"May we have a proper look around the ship, please?" Alice-Miranda gazed up with her brown eyes as big as saucers. "I promise we won't touch anything we shouldn't and we won't get in anyone's way."

"Aren't you just the most precious child for asking?" Aunty Gee beamed at Granny Valentina. "Of course, Alice-Miranda, you can explore wherever you like, my dear—perhaps except the engine room—I fear it might be a little dangerous down there. Otherwise, just make sure that you turn up on time for meals and the ship is yours for the whole voyage. And who are you going to do your sightseeing with?"

Alice-Miranda beckoned to the other children, who were milling about behind Granny Bert and her beautiful granddaughter Daisy, who often helped Cecelia out at home.

{56}

"Aunty Gee, do you remember my good friend Millie?" Millie stepped forward and curtsied as awkwardly as she had the first time she'd met Aunty Gee at Highton Hall.

"Dear, I'd remember that curtsy anywhere. You thought I was Mrs. Oliver's sister," Aunty Gee replied. "And look at dear Dolly over there today—it's no wonder you thought we were related. I'd say she's more my twin than anyone else on earth."

Millie's paprika freckles looked like they'd just caught fire, and she managed a small grin.

"And this is my friend Jacinta Headlington-Bear." Alice-Miranda urged Jacinta forward.

"You're the gymnast, aren't you?" Aunty Gee asked.

Jacinta beamed, thrilled to be remembered.

"And you know Lucas, Uncle Lawrence's son." Lucas stepped forward. Aunty Gee held out her hand, which Lucas gently took in his and then bowed.

"Oh, you little charmer. Just like your father." Aunty Gee blushed.

"And this is Sep Sykes. He's Lucas's roommate at Fayle," Alice-Miranda said. Sep hung back a little until Millie gave him an enthusiastic shove forward, causing him to bump into Aunty Gee.

"I am so sorry, Your Majesty." Sep wanted to dissolve into the floor.

Aunty Gee waved her hand. "Oh, don't be silly, lad. That's nothing compared to the treatment I get from those grandchildren of mine. Regard me like a hobby horse, climbing all over me, they do. It's lovely to meet you, Sep. Welcome aboard the *Octavia*."

"Alice-Miranda," her mother called. "Are you going to take Annie and Poppy with you too?"

"I haven't seen them," Alice-Miranda replied.

"Oh, I know where they are, dear," Granny Valentina piped up. "I saw Lady Sarah and Lord Robert taking the girls to their suite. You know Sarah suffers terribly with seasickness. It's awfully strange— poor girl turns green on arrival—I've seen it before. But after a day or so she seems to get her sea legs and she's fine. Robert mentioned that the youngsters were feeling peaky too, so it must be in the genes."

"Oh." Alice-Miranda frowned. "I hope they feel better soon."

"Well, off you go!" Aunty Gee waved. "Have a wonderful time, and don't take any nonsense from the crew. They're a scurrilous lot." She winked at Admiral Harding, who was within earshot talking to Hugh and Lawrence.

Alice-Miranda, Millie, Jacinta, Lucas and Sep gathered together in the corner of the deck.

"Where will we go first?" Lucas asked the group.

"Maybe Admiral Harding will have a plan of the ship we can borrow," Sep suggested.

"It's much more fun exploring without one," Millie replied. "Besides, the *Octavia*'s not that huge, is she?"

"No," Alice-Miranda agreed. "Mummy said that the *Octavia* is not nearly as big as some of the other liners. I think there's accommodation for around three hundred guests with another two hundred fifty crew."

Sep raised his eyebrows. "Still, it's not exactly a rowboat."

Built just on thirty years ago, to exacting standards, the Royal Yacht *Octavia* was a sublime example of the best quality craftsmanship, from her polished decks to the maple wood paneling that lined the inside passageways. A recent refurbishment had ensured that she was still state-of-the-art. There was a main dining room and two smaller areas for more casual eating, an oak-paneled library with crystal chandeliers and a stunning drawing room, complete with grand piano, comfy couches and a cabinet full of glittering jeweled Fabergé eggs—apparently a gift from the last tsar of Russia to Aunty Gee's grandmother many years ago. The grandest room on the ship was the ballroom, which could accommodate all three hundred guests and had an enormous dance floor. This would play host to several events on the voyage, including a Bollywood theme night and a pre-wedding formal dinner and, of course, the wedding itself, which would take place on the last night of the cruise.

On the upper decks there were opulent apartment-like suites, with an entrance hall, sitting room, bedroom, full bathroom and a balcony, while the suites on the lower levels were slightly smaller and not quite as luxurious.

"Is there a pool?" Jacinta asked.

"I think so." Alice-Miranda nodded. "Mummy said it was on the upper deck and it's fully enclosed with glass—so we can still swim if the weather turns."

"I expect that's where I'm most likely to find my mother," Jacinta decided.

"Well, come on, let's go and see." And with that, Millie led the charge up a narrow flight of stairs.

Chapter 9

An hour later the children were quite lost. They'd seen the upper and middle decks, found the pool but not Jacinta's mother, and now downstairs was proving more of a labyrinth than they'd imagined.

"I wonder what's through there?" said Alice-Miranda. The children pushed open an ornate set of double doors and emerged into the most splendid ballroom. It was encased in highly polished burr walnut paneling, with a vast parquetry floor and sparkling chandeliers. Alice-Miranda found herself imagining what it would look like for Aunt Charlotte and Lawrence's wedding.

"Wow, this is some room," Lucas marveled. In the far corner a man with a gravity-defying brown Afro hairstyle emerged from a side storeroom, carrying a music stand in each hand.

Alice-Miranda led her friends toward him. The man was humming to himself and seemed unaware of their approach. As they drew closer Alice-Miranda could hear tinny music as well as the humming and realized that underneath all that hair the man must have been wearing earphones.

"Excuse me. Hello." She tapped him on the arm. The man leapt sideways, startled by the ambush. He dropped the two stands, which clattered to the floor.

"You scared me half to death," he breathed, pulling the earphones from his ears and switching off his player. "What did you do that for?"

"I'm terribly sorry, sir. I didn't mean to alarm you. My name's Alice-Miranda Highton-Smith-Kennington-Jones and I'm very pleased to meet you." She held out her hand.

"Well, I couldn't say the same. What are you doing in here?" the man asked as he stared at Alice-Miranda and her friends, ignoring her outstretched hand.

"Well, we've been exploring all over the ship and now we're a little bit lost. These are my friends Millie and Jacinta and Lucas and Septimus, but you can call him Sep."

The man frowned. "Well, there's nothing for you to see in here. Just a big empty ballroom, that's all."

"Do you have a name, sir?" Alice-Miranda asked.

"Of course." He stared at her. "It's Alex. Now you'd better run along. Don't want your parents to worry, do you?"

"Oh, they're not worried at all. And we checked with Aunty Gee and she said that we could go exploring anywhere we liked," Alice-Miranda replied.

"Really?" he said, glowering.

"What's through there?" Millie asked, pointing at the doorway from which the man had emerged.

"Just a storeroom," Alex answered.

"Do you need a hand?" Lucas asked, looking at the music stands.

"Are you setting up for the band?" said Alice-Miranda. "We could help you."

"Yes, for rehearsal, but I don't need any help. The others will be along soon." Alex wasn't used to children, and he didn't appreciate the persistence of this lot.

"Are you *in* the band with Mr. Morrison?" Alice-Miranda asked. "What do you play?"

The man gave a half nod and said, "Saxophone."

"I love the saxophone. It's got such a smooth sound." Alice-Miranda smiled.

"Can we have a look in there?" Millie asked, already making her way toward the storeroom.

Before Alex had time to protest, Millie called out to her friends, "You should see this. There are so many instruments. This must be an enormous band."

The children charged over to see what Millie was marveling at.

"I used to play the trumpet," said Lucas, picking up a somewhat tatty leather case with a smiley-face sticker on the side.

"Put that down," Alex demanded.

"I was just going to have a look," Lucas replied. "I wouldn't play it."

"No, you certainly will not! Put it down. Nobody's allowed to touch that case," he snapped.

"Okay, keep your hair on," Lucas whispered as he placed the case back on the ground next to the forty or so others of various shapes and sizes.

Jacinta giggled.

"Well, it's been nice to meet you, Mr. Alex. I can't wait to see you in the band." Alice-Miranda smiled.

"The door's that way." Alex pointed. His face was stony and his eyes had taken on a rather dark hue.

"Come on," Sep said. "Let's leave the man to do his work."

"Goodbye, Mr. Alex," said Alice-Miranda with a final smile before she skipped after her friends, who were already halfway out the door.

"What is it with people on this ship?" Jacinta griped when the children were on the other side of the door.

"What do you mean?" Alice-Miranda asked.

"Well, Alex didn't exactly seem pleased to see us, and I think Mr. Winterstone hates us. And they've both got weird hair."

"That's silly. I'm sure Mr. Alex was just busy, and Mr. Winterstone is perfectly lovely. I don't think many children come on board the *Octavia*. Maybe the staff just aren't used to having kids around," Alice-Miranda said.

The children had exited the ballroom through a different door from the one they had gone in and found themselves in yet another unfamiliar passageway.

"What do you think's through there?" Millie pointed at a door she hoped would lead them back upstairs.

"Who knows? But there's no harm in looking." Alice-Miranda led the group through the heavy metal door. A delicious smell wafted in the air, teasing the group's grumbling stomachs.

"I think we must be somewhere near the kitchen," said Jacinta.

"Genius." Lucas rolled his eyes. Jacinta thumped him gently on the arm in response.

"Well, who's hungry?" Alice-Miranda asked. "Maybe we can get something to eat."

The children followed a passageway lined on either side with giant refrigerators.

A young man with glassy eyes appeared from inside one of the cool rooms, carrying a box of lettuce. He didn't speak but pushed his way past the children through a clear plastic flap at the end of the corridor. The children could see into a galley kitchen, where several men were handling large knives and one appeared to be using a blowtorch.

"It looks a bit crazy in there," said Sep. He didn't like the thought of interrupting the chefs while they were busy *and* armed.

"Kitchens are always like that," Alice-Miranda reassured him. "We can just say hello and then perhaps someone can help us find our way back upstairs again."

Alice-Miranda poked her head around the plastic flap. "Hello?" she called. But no one paid her the slightest bit of attention. She pushed her way into the kitchen and motioned for her friends to follow.

Once inside, the children could see they were standing in a narrow passageway adjacent to the main part of the kitchen. Two men were furiously chopping rhubarb while another, the one with the blowtorch, was putting the finishing touches to some crème brûlées.

The children might as well have been invisible.

"These guys are really focused." Lucas looked around and wondered for a moment if the chefs were actually human.

"Yes. Are you sure they're not robots?" Jacinta giggled.

"Mind reader." Lucas grinned—and Jacinta melted.

Farther along, the passageway opened up into a full commercial kitchen—enormous by any standards and at least twice the size of Mrs. Smith's space at Winchesterfield-Downsfordvale.

Alice-Miranda counted over twenty men, resplendent in their white uniforms and mushroom-shaped hats, all busily chopping and braising and whipping—apparently oblivious to their presence. It was a strange scene indeed. Alice-Miranda had been a guest in many a large kitchen in her seven and three-quarter years, but never had she seen anything quite like this.

She had a strange feeling about this place—and

Alice-Miranda was usually right about her strange feelings. Something wasn't right. There was no noise, other than the sound of utensils.

"You need to go," a tiny voice whispered. Alice-Miranda looked around to see who had spoken.

"Hello." She smiled at a young man who was chopping onions. "My name is Alice-Miranda Highton-Smith-Kennington-Jones and I'm very pleased to meet you."

The chef looked at her and shook his head ever so slightly. "Miss, you must go—and take your friends with you," he said through gritted teeth.

Alice-Miranda glanced around the room. There didn't seem to be anyone in charge, which she thought very strange. There was always a head chef. They were often renowned for their bad tempers, but Alice-Miranda had met enough of them to know that they were mostly pussycats outside the kitchen. After all, she reasoned, cooking for hundreds of guests was probably about one of the most stressful jobs anyone could have.

"Alice-Miranda, maybe we *should* just leave?" Millie suggested. She noticed that the longer they stayed, the redder the faces on the chefs became, as though the children's mere presence was raising the temperature in the room.

"It's all right," Alice-Miranda assured her friend. She turned to address the young chef, who was still chopping onions. "Excuse me, sir, can you tell us who is in charge?"

The man sniffed. Moisture which had dammed in the corners of his eyes spilled over, streaming down his tanned cheeks.

"Are you all right?" She reached into her pocket and handed him a clean tissue.

He motioned at the onions on the bench.

"Oh, of course." Alice-Miranda smiled. "I don't like chopping onions either. Mrs. Oliver is working on a 'no tears' variety at the moment, but I don't know if she's made much progress yet."

"Come on, let's get out of here," Lucas directed.

All at once there was a whooshing noise, like an approaching freight train. The chefs, already working at a rate of knots, seemed to flick their speed dials to "overdrive."

Into the kitchen blew a tornado, through which a veritable giant emerged. At least six feet five inches tall, with shoulders the width of a doorway, a chiseled jaw, jet-black hair and eyes that looked like they could pierce steel, he surveyed the activity in front of him and proceeded to explode.

"What iz that?" the titan roared at one young fellow

who was whipping cream. His forefinger, the size of a pork sausage, plunged into the vat of frothy white liquid and flew back into his open mouth. "That . . . iz contaminated." He picked up the bowl and promptly upended it on the young man's head.

He moved along the line. "And what are those?" he growled. The chef gulped. "Well? Tell me!" the giant commanded.

"Prawns, Chef," the young man squeaked as he stared at a tub full of plump orange crustaceans.

"Who bring prawns on board ship? I have list of banned foods. The Queen Georgiana iz allergic to all shellfish and crustaceans. You want me to kill Queen? Do you? Do you?" he demanded.

"No, Chef." The young man trembled.

"Well, take them and throw them overboard!"

By now Millie, Jacinta, Lucas and Sep had inched backward around the corner into the narrow passageway, where they were willing themselves to be invisible. Only Alice-Miranda stayed put.

The tyrant paced among the cooks, who had begun to resemble a row of trembling jellyfish.

"That fish . . . ," he roared, then picked up a large boning knife, plunging it into the chopping board and just missing the creature's head . . . "iz dead!"

"Thank goodness for that." Lucas smirked. The other children giggled.

"What waz that?" the giant bellowed. "Who iz in my kitchen?"

"Isn't that line from a fairy tale?" Millie whispered.

"Yes—and didn't those kids end up in an oven?" Sep gulped.

Alice-Miranda strode toward the colossus. "Hello, my name is Alice-Miranda Highton-Smith-Kennington-Jones and I'm very pleased to meet you."

"She's done for." Lucas covered his eyes as his cousin-to-be reached out her tiny hand.

"Who said that?" the giant replied.

"Me, sir. Down here. You see, you're ever so tall and I'm really quite tiny, so it would help if you looked down," Alice-Miranda suggested.

The giant lowered his eyes. He raised his left paw to his forehead.

"Oh no! He's going to crush her," Millie squeaked.

Then he ran his fingers slowly through his hair.

"What you doing in my kitchen?" he demanded.

"Aunty Gee gave us permission to have a look around the ship and, well, we got a little bit lost and that's when we found the kitchen. Do you know from out in that corridor it smells like roasting meat and baking potatoes and the best of Mrs. Oliver's cakes all rolled into one? My stomach almost did a back-flip. I'm rather hungry after all our exploring. But I must say, sir, you have the quietest kitchen I've ever been in. Your chefs are very attentive."

"Aunty Gee, you zay she gave you run of ship. Who is Gee?" He looked perplexed.

"Oh, you probably know her as Queen Georgiana. But I call her Aunty Gee. She's Mummy's and Aunt Charlotte's godmother and my Granny Valentina's best friend since nursery school," Alice-Miranda explained.

"The Queen Georgiana, she iz your aunt?" he asked.

"Well, not really, not by blood, but that doesn't matter because I adore her just the same—and I think she's quite fond of Mummy and Aunt Charlotte and me too."

The giant looked around. The other chefs had slowed down considerably and were watching the action from the corners of their eyes.

"Get on with it!" he roared.

The chefs went back to their whisking and whipping and whizzing quick-smart.

"And you are close to Queen?" he asked.

"Oh yes, very close. We almost always see her

at Christmas and for birthdays," Alice-Miranda prattled. "And another couple of times at least throughout the year. I didn't catch your name, sir," Alice-Miranda finished, gazing up at him.

"I am Vladimir." He raised his nose in the air and stood like a proud rooster.

"Do you have a surname, Mr. Vladimir?" Alice-Miranda asked.

He stepped back. "No, no surname. I don't need one."

Alice-Miranda smiled. "Well then, I'll call you Chef Vladimir. Now tell me, that accent of yours, it's rather lovely. Is it Russian, by any chance?"

Vladimir gazed at this tiny child with her cascading chocolate curls and eyes as big as saucers and wondered if she was real.

"Yez, I am Rrrrusky and prrroud," he replied with perfect rolling Rs.

The other children, hearing the exchange, began to emerge from their hiding spot.

"And who are you?" Vladimir demanded as he caught sight of the foursome. His tone sent Jacinta scurrying behind Millie.

"These are my good friends, Millie, Jacinta, Lucas and Septimus, but he prefers Sep." Alice-Miranda waved her hand, urging them forward.

"Well, get out of my kitchen. No children allowed. Out!"

Millie, Jacinta, Sep and Lucas were gone before he'd finished his bellowing. Only Alice-Miranda stayed behind.

"I am looking forward to eating your delicious food, Chef Vladimir. Perhaps we'll see you again tomorrow." She waved and skipped off to find her friends.

Vladimir thumped his plate-sized fist onto the steel bench. No one had told him there would be children on board. In his opinion, children were akin to rats: dirty, smelly little troublemakers. There was no doubt that the world would be better off without them. He would need to make sure that this one, who seemed rather persistent, would not cause any problems and upset his grand plans for the week.

Chapter 10

"I was so scared." Jacinta breathed deeply when the children were safely out of the kitchen and back on deck.

"Vladimir certainly has an interesting management style," Sep observed.

"Well, I'm sure he's a wonderful chef," Alice-Miranda enthused. "There were some delicious smells in that kitchen."

"We thought he was going to squish you under his hairy paw," said Millie, "and then roast us all in the ovens and serve us for dinner tonight."

The children looked at each other and gulped. Only Alice-Miranda smiled.

"Hello." Cecelia walked over and interrupted the group. "So where have you lot been?"

"Hello, Mummy. We've had the most wonderful afternoon exploring the ship. We saw the pool and the library and the ballroom and the kitchen," Alice-Miranda told her.

"And we met the scariest chef in the world," Jacinta added.

"Mr. Rodgers?" Cecelia raised her eyebrows. "I've known him since I was ten years old. He doesn't have a frightening bone in his body. You know his nickname is Jolly."

"Well, this man's name certainly isn't Jolly. It's Vladimir, and he's a giant and especially fierce with his staff," Jacinta said.

Cecelia Highton-Smith called to her sister, Charlotte, who was standing nearby talking with Daisy and Granny Bert.

"Cha, excuse me, darling, what happened to Mr. Rodgers?"

"Oh, poor fellow has a broken leg. It was a dreadful accident—a hit-and-run on the high street a few weeks ago. Admiral Harding said Mr. Rodgers simply didn't see the car. I can't believe the driver didn't stop—poor man could have been killed. He wanted to do the wedding, but I told Aunty Gee that would be terribly unfair. I couldn't imagine him hopping about down there on crutches. So Lawrence organized another chef through a friend of his. The man's a bit of a celebrity in Russia—stunning food, but not known for his patience. Apparently he's been dying to cook for Aunty Gee for ages—increase his prestige at home and all. He insisted on bringing some of his own team too."

"We met him a little while ago," Alice-Miranda piped up.

"And you're right about him being impatient. His staff are terrified of him," Lucas added.

"I'm sure he's not as bad as all that," Alice-Miranda insisted. "Chefs are just focused, that's all."

Cecelia glanced up and caught sight of Millie's mother and father talking with Mrs. Oliver and Ambrose.

"Did you see your parents, Jacinta?" Cecelia asked. She wondered where on earth they could have got to. Everyone else had managed to make it up on deck to push off, and since then most of the guests had been milling about chatting, taking tea and having a lovely catch-up.

"No." Jacinta frowned.

"Never mind, they're probably just taking a while to get settled. I'm sure they'll be up shortly," Cecelia said reassuringly. She secretly wondered if she'd done the right thing inviting them. It didn't seem fair that Millie should have her family on board when Jacinta would have no one. Cecelia had been surprised when she received word (at the very last minute) that the Headlington-Bears would attend and had requested two suites. But at least Jacinta would get to spend some time with them.

When the children hadn't found Ambrosia by the pool, Jacinta had decided not to worry about her mother and father. She had no idea what they'd talk about when she did see them. Of course Charlotte and Lawrence were terribly kind inviting her parents, but really it would have suited her just as well if they'd stayed away. She had a sinking feeling that they most likely only agreed to come because of Lawrence and the possibility of meeting some of his movie-star friends.

The late-afternoon sun was playing hide-and-seek with the clouds. The children were keen to test the pool before dark and had decided on their way back from the kitchen to see if they might have a swim before nightfall.

Lucas asked Charlotte if that was all right.

"Of course," she replied. "Just don't be late for dinner."

"Okay, let's meet at the pool in ten minutes," Jacinta instructed as the children headed to their suites to get changed.

"All right, but I might be a little longer," said Alice-Miranda. "There's something I need to do first."

Chapter 11

Alice-Miranda marched off to the bridge to see if Admiral Harding could tell her which suite Jacinta's parents were staying in. She was keen to find them and see if everything was all right.

"Hello?" she called, and knocked.

She could hear voices on the other side of the door.

"Hello?" She tried again, and then pushed the door open.

A control panel of blinking lights sat beneath panoramic windows overlooking the bow of the ship. In the center of the console an empty chair sat in front of what looked like a joystick. Two men were standing on the opposite side of the room.

"You don't want to give me any more reasons to speak with the admiral, do you?" the taller man asked.

"Of course not, sir." The shorter man shook his head.

"Well then, I'm sure you can follow some very simple instructions, can't you?" The other man raised his eyebrows.

"Excuse me," Alice-Miranda said. "I'm very sorry to disturb you, but I was looking for Admiral Harding."

"Go," the taller man instructed the shorter one. "I will speak to you later."

The shorter man sped from the room, ignoring Alice-Miranda completely. She noticed that his face was the color of beetroot and he kept his head down as he exited. She had a strange feeling that something wasn't quite right. The poor man looked as though he'd been caught with his hand in the cookie jar.

"May I help you?" the taller man offered.

"Oh, I hope so," Alice-Miranda replied. "My name's Alice-Miranda Highton-Smith-Kennington-Jones and I'm very pleased to meet you Mr. . . . ."

"Prendergast, First Officer, ah . . . Whitley Prendergast," the man replied.

"Well, it's lovely to meet you, First Officer

Prendergast, and this is such a delicious view." She stared out at the sea. "I'm sorry to have interrupted your meeting before."

"He just made a mistake," Whitley replied, "which will be repaid in due course."

Alice-Miranda wondered what the other man must have done. Her frown betrayed her thoughts.

"But nothing for you to worry about, miss." Prendergast walked to the other side of the room and took a clipboard from the wall.

"Oh, of course not," Alice-Miranda replied. "You must adore working on the *Octavia*."

"Yes," Prendergast agreed.

"It must be so much fun to travel the world instead of being locked away—"

Prendergast glared. "What do you mean, 'locked away'?"

"In an office," Alice-Miranda explained. "Working in the same place every day."

"Oh, indeed." Prendergast roared laughing.

"Do you get to steer the ship?" Alice-Miranda asked.

"Yes, miss."

"But who's doing that now?" Alice-Miranda walked around the empty seat in front of the middle of the control panel. "I thought you would have loads of help up here—it's amazing to have a huge vessel like the *Octavia* and only one person in control. You must be very good at your job."

"Autopilot. But I'm sure you didn't come just to admire the view and talk about my work," he prompted.

"Oh no, of course not. I wondered if you could help me locate some of our guests. My friend Jacinta Headlington-Bear's parents are on board but she hasn't seen them yet, and I just want to make sure that they're all right."

Whitley Prendergast walked to the other side of the room and thumbed through a thick folder.

"Here they are." He tapped his finger on the page.

"Headlington-Bear—Victoria and Albert. On the Gallery Deck," Prendergast informed her.

"Thank you, Mr. Prendergast," Alice-Miranda said. "I'm sure I'll find them."

She turned to leave.

The child glanced back at Prendergast and waved. "Enjoy your evening."

But the first officer did not reply. He was humming loudly and seemed rather focused on cutting up some paper.

People who work on ships are very busy, Alice-Miranda thought.

She made her way down five flights of stairs to the Gallery Deck, so named for the millions of dollars' worth of artwork that lined the long corridors; Picassos and Rembrandts hung alongside works by Matisse and Monet. It was a truly splendid hallway, despite being belowdecks. She walked along the corridor, checking the polished brass nameplates in the center of each door.

"Ah, here it is, Victoria Suite," Alice-Miranda said. "That's funny—I thought it was Victoria and Albert." Alice-Miranda wondered if she was in the right place. It was definitely the Gallery Deck—it said so at the end of the hall. She tapped on the door lightly. There was no reply, so she waited a moment, then tapped again more firmly.

Ambrosia Headlington-Bear, having made no decision about her outfit for the ship's departure, had retreated to the bath, where she lay under a froth of bubbles. With some soothing jazz in her ears, she wondered how on earth she was going to choose what to wear for dinner.

"Well," said Alice-Miranda with a shrug, "perhaps they've gone upstairs."

Inside the Albert Suite opposite, Neville Nordstrom's stomach grumbled. No one else had come to claim the room, so he'd decided that he might as well stay put for now—except that he really needed something to eat. He'd drifted off to sleep again after being awoken by the blasting of the ship's horn when the vessel was casting off. And now he'd been here for what seemed a couple of hours. Considering he'd lain awake most of the night before, worrying about the journey ahead, it was no surprise that Neville was tired.

Neville decided to go in search of some food—surely there had to be a vending machine or cafeteria somewhere close by. He picked up his trumpet case and opened the door. A small girl with cascading chocolate curls was standing outside in the hallway. Neville stepped backward and closed the door. He hoped she would go away.

Alice-Miranda spun around to see who was there. But the door had clicked shut. And then she saw the nameplate—ALBERT SUITE.

"Oh, so that's it! The Headlington-Bears must have two suites," Alice-Miranda decided.

Knowing there was someone inside, she knocked sharply at the door and waited.

Neville stood on the other side wondering what he should do.

"Hello," Alice-Miranda called. "Is anyone there?"

Neville felt his chest tighten. She must have seen him.

Alice-Miranda waited a moment and then rapped sharply again. "Hello. Are you there?"

Neville opened the door.

"Oh, hello." Alice-Miranda smiled. "My name's Alice-Miranda Highton-Smith-Kennington-Jones and I'm very pleased to meet you." She thrust a dainty hand toward him.

Neville's eyes were cast toward the floor.

"Are you all right?" Alice-Miranda asked.

Neville nodded but didn't look up. He didn't know what to do. He didn't like girls. They made him nervous.

"Mmm," he mumbled.

"I'm looking for my friend Jacinta Headlington-Bear's parents, and I thought they were in the Victoria and Albert Suite but I think I must have made a mistake and perhaps they have two suites, the Victoria *and* the Albert, but you're here, so I think First Officer Prendergast must have misread the passenger list. Oh! Do you play the trumpet?" Alice-Miranda asked, glancing toward his case.

Neville moved his head ever so slightly.

"Oh, that's wonderful! Do you know that there's an

old-fashioned big band on board? Their leader is Mr. Morrison, and he's the most amazing trumpet player ever. I saw all their instruments before when my friends and I were exploring the ship. I can't wait to hear them play. Maybe they'll let you practice with them, or perhaps if you're really good, which you must be to have brought your instrument on board with you, you might even be able to play with them."

Neville had no idea what to say. So he said nothing.

"Do you have a name?" Alice-Miranda asked.

Neville gulped. His mouth felt like he'd swallowed a bucket of sand.

"Neville," he whispered.

"Well, it's lovely to have met you, Neville. Would you like to come and meet my friends? We're going swimming," Alice-Miranda enthused. "The pool's heated."

He glanced at his case and then flicked his gaze back to her momentarily.

"Oh, are you off to do some practice? Well, that's lovely. I do hope I might see you at dinner tonight. I'm sure my friends would love to meet you too."

Neville chewed at the quick at the base of his thumbnail and gripped the handle of his battered case. He wished this girl would disappear.

"Well, I've got to get back upstairs. I hope I see you later." Alice-Miranda skipped down the passage.

Neville rather hoped he never saw her again. He stepped backward into the room, closed the door and took a deep breath. He was cross with himself. If only he hadn't been so jolly tongue-tied, he could have asked her where he could find something to eat. She seemed to know everything. There was another sharp knock at the door and a young man in a white uniform entered.

"Oh, good afternoon, sir." The man almost walked straight into him. "I see you're awake. Would you like me to bring you anything? I looked in earlier and you were sound asleep."

Neville was frozen to the spot. He did not reply.

"Might I inquire where you are heading off to, sir?" The man looked at Neville's case. "I must say I've never seen anyone quite so devoted to their luggage."

Neville didn't return his smile. "I-i-is . . . is this my room?" he mumbled.

"I should think so, sir. You are Master Neville?"

Neville nodded ever so slightly.

"Would you like some help to unpack, sir?" The young man went to take the case from Neville's hand.

"No." Neville spun around. "I-i-it's okay. I—I've got it."

"Well then, at least allow me to bring you something to eat. Is there anything particular you'd like?"

Neville shuffled back through the open doorway into the entrance hall and then across into the sitting room. He walked over and sat on the couch, dragging his case onto his lap.

"Ham s-s-sandwich," he whispered.

"Very good, sir. Would you like mustard and some French fries with that?"

Neville's stomach grumbled.

"I should think so," the steward said. "My name is Henderson, sir, and I will be looking after you for the week. My apologies that I wasn't here to meet you when you arrived. I had some unexpected business to attend to, but I'm here now, and I'm sure everything will be smooth sailing from here on in."

Neville stared at the floor.

"Very good, Master Neville." The steward exited the room.

Neville heaved a deep sigh. At least he could settle in properly, knowing he was in the right place.

Neville was yet to discover, wedged between the writing desk and the bookshelf, his welcome letter addressed to Mr. Neville Headlington-Bear.

Chapter 12

"Oh, there you are, darling." Cecelia Highton-Smith had glanced up from where she was sitting by the pool, talking to their gardener, Harold Greening, and his wife, Maggie, to see her daughter skipping toward them. "Where have you been? The others have been in for ages. You've only got a few minutes and then we have to get ready for dinner."

"Sorry, Mummy, I wanted to check that Mr. and Mrs. Headlington-Bear were all right, and then I had to get my bathers on," Alice-Miranda called.

"Did you see them, darling?" Cecelia asked.

"No, I think they must have already come up for drinks," Alice-Miranda replied.

Cecelia Highton-Smith glanced around the open deck. "I haven't spied them yet, but they might be inside. I'll go and have a look."

Most of the guests had retreated to their suites to change for dinner. The sun blinked its last warm rays before slipping down behind the mountains. Alice-Miranda pulled her dress over her head. She closed her eyes, jumped into the pool and was embraced by the warm water.

"Where have you been?" Millie shouted. Alice-Miranda swam over to join her friends.

"I just had to check on something," Alice-Miranda replied.

The children played a quick round of Marco Polo before Cecelia reappeared and said it was time to have showers and get ready for dinner.

"Do we have to dress up tonight, Mummy?" Alice-Miranda asked as she toweled herself off.

"No, darling. We're having a barbecue on the Royal Deck—you can keep the formal wear in the wardrobe until later in the week."

"So that's what smells so delicious," Lucas said, sniffing the air appreciatively.

"You know, I think being on a ship is the perfect holiday for kids," Millie observed. "The grown-ups don't have to worry about us at all—we can't get lost, or kidnapped, or anything."

"True," said Jacinta. "But bad luck if there's someone on board you don't want to see. You're bound to meet up with them at some stage."

Alice-Miranda and Millie exchanged knowing looks. They both wondered how Jacinta's parents could be on the ship and still not have bothered to seek out their daughter. It simply wasn't right.

"Well, off you go. You'll need to be back up on deck in half an hour for dinner," Cecelia commanded.

"Will you be joining the other guests on deck for dinner this evening, sir?" Henderson asked as he cleared the empty tray. Neville had devoured his ham sandwich and French fries and left nothing behind at all—quite a feat for a young boy. "It's a barbecue, and I've heard the new chef's a real star. I hope there'll be leftovers for the crew."

Neville didn't know what to say. It wasn't in his nature to talk to strangers. It wasn't in his nature to talk to anyone very much.

He vaguely shook his head.

"Very well, sir. Would you like me to bring you a plate in an hour or so?"

He nodded and wished Henderson would stop yapping.

"I think there's going to be fireworks later tonight too."

Henderson wondered about Neville. Painfully shy wouldn't go halfway to describing the poor lad. Certainly he was the polar opposite of his gossipy mother across the hallway. She never stopped talking and asking Henderson's opinion on which dress looked best and how she should do her hair. You'd have thought the woman had never got dressed on her own before.

"Do you play?" Henderson looked at the trumpet case tucked in beside Neville on the couch. Its brown leather trim had seen more than a few bumps and knocks, and there was a rather large smiley-face sticker in the middle of the lid.

Neville nodded. He found nodding was the best way to answer most questions.

"May I have a look, Master Neville?" Henderson asked.

Neville shook his head. "No, it's nothing special," he whispered.

"Oh well, perhaps I'll have the pleasure of hearing you practice," Henderson suggested.

"I . . . I . . . only play for me. It's private."

"Oh, okay, sir." Henderson frowned. Having played trombone for years in his own school band, Henderson thought that was very odd indeed. Playing a brass or woodwind instrument without others was a bit like being the defense, attack and goalie on the soccer team. You didn't stand a hope, really, and in his experience it wasn't much fun at all.

Chapter 13

The Royal Deck had been completely transformed for dinner. Fairy lights twinkled along the railings, and large Chinese lanterns swayed above, suspended from slender cables. The section of deck set for dinner was enclosed and heated, keeping the chill breath of the ocean at bay. Thirty round tables, resplendent with white cloths, sparkling candelabra and silverware so highly polished you could clean your teeth in its reflection, adorned the rear of the ship. A row of gleaming barbecues groaned under the weight of their sizzling feasts.

Alice-Miranda, Millie and Jacinta were escorted to their table by a handsome steward. The girls were sitting with Lucas and Sep and wondered who else might join them. Cecelia and Hugh were dining with Granny Valentina, Aunty Gee, Lawrence, Charlotte, Mrs. Oliver, Millie's grandfather and Shilly. Over by the dance floor, a small musical ensemble struck up a tune, adding to the festive mood.

"Hold on a tick, I'd better say hello to Mum and Dad." Millie excused herself and walked over to see her parents, who were seated at the admiral's table with Daisy and Granny Bert, Mr. and Mrs. Greening and some other guests she didn't recognize.

Jacinta glanced around the deck.

"Still haven't spotted them?" Alice-Miranda asked.

"No," said Jacinta. "But it's typical. Mummy's probably caught up on the telephone." She shrugged. "And Daddy will be busy doing some billion-dollar deal."

"I'm sure they'll be here soon," Alice-Miranda reassured her.

A tinkling of silver on crystal signified the formal start of the meal. Admiral Harding stood up and cleared his throat.

"Ahem. Good evening, Your Majesty, my lords, ladies and gentlemen, what a pleasure it is to have you here on board the *Octavia* for what will be a most wonderful voyage. Our gracious hostess, Queen Georgiana, has requested that royal protocol be kept to a minimum as we are here to celebrate the impending marriage of Miss Charlotte Highton-Smith to the most charming and soon to be not-so-eligible bachelor, star of stage and screen Mr. Lawrence Ridley."

"Hear, hear." Ambrose McLoughlin-McTavish raised his glass.

"I couldn't agree more." Aunty Gee held her champagne flute aloft.

"Before we partake of this most tantalizing meal, I'd like to let you know a little about the route we'll be taking this week. The *Octavia* has this afternoon been sailing along the French Riviera. We will be continuing on to the Italian Riviera and the Amalfi Coast before traveling up the Adriatic Sea to our point of disembarkation in the magical city of Venice. Although there are some glorious ports along the way, I'm sure you can appreciate that it is Charlotte and Lawrence's wish that we remain on board until the end of the cruise, and so, while we will admire from afar, we won't be stopping in. Buzzing helicopters and long lenses are not something any of us want to attract to this celebration."

A titter of laughter rang around the deck.

"So, may I propose a toast? Will you please stand? To our happy couple, Charlotte and Lawrence."

The chorus reverberated around the deck. "Charlotte and Lawrence."

"I hope you all enjoy your meal, and I look forward to meeting many of you on the dance floor a little later in the evening."

The tempting smell of barbecued meat and salty air wafted across the deck as a conga line of wait-staff began depositing plates of food in front of the eager diners.

"Look, there's Chef Vladimir." Alice-Miranda spied a giant in a tall white hat presiding over the chefs. Standing beside him was a raven-haired beauty. Her bejeweled kaftan caught the lantern glow from above, sending shards of soft light across her pretty face. Millie nudged Alice-Miranda.

Jacinta swiveled her head to see what Millie and Alice-Miranda were looking at. Just as quickly, she spun back around and gave her fullest concentration to the fillet of beef on the plate in front of her.

"Jacinta, isn't that your mother?" Millie pointed at the woman. Although Millie had never met her in person, she'd seen enough photographs of Ambrosia Headlington-Bear to know that it had to be her.

"Yes, I suspect it is." Jacinta plowed into her potato.

In a second, Alice-Miranda was out of her seat and charging toward the woman.

"Good evening, Chef Vladimir." Alice-Miranda smiled at the head chef. "It's lovely to see you again, and this barbecue smells delicious."

"Of courze it doez," he sneered.

"Excuse me, but are you Mrs. Headlington-Bear?" she asked.

"Yes, of course I'm Ambrosia Headlington-Bear," the woman replied.

"Oh, thank goodness," said Alice-Miranda. "I was wondering if you were really on board the ship at all."

The woman stared blankly at Alice-Miranda.

"I am sorry. I haven't even introduced myself. My name is Alice-Miranda Highton-Smith-Kennington-Jones and I'm so very pleased to finally meet you." Alice-Miranda thrust her tiny hand in Ambrosia's direction.

"Oh." Ambrosia studied the child for a moment before taking her hand into her limp grip. "Oh!" she said again, a tiny flicker of recognition igniting on her face.

"My mummy and daddy invited you. Well, Aunt Charlotte and Uncle Lawrence actually insisted that you be invited," Alice-Miranda continued. "Jacinta is one of my best friends."

"What's Jacinta got to do with all this?" Ambrosia attempted to furrow her brow, but it steadfastly refused to budge.

"Well, Mummy and Daddy thought it would be lovely if I could have Jacinta and Millie along on the cruise, and then Aunt Charlotte and Uncle Lawrence said that it would be great to meet their parents, and that's how you and Mr. Headlington-Bear and Millie's mother and father came to be asked too."

"But I was invited because I *always* get invited to these things," Ambrosia said, puzzled.

"Well, I imagine that you do get invited to loads of things, but this time you really do have Jacinta to thank," Alice-Miranda replied.

"So my daughter's here, on the ship?" Ambrosia pouted.

"Oh yes. She's just over there." Alice-Miranda pointed toward the children at the table. "She'll be so relieved about the mix-up. I think Jacinta had begun to wonder if you were avoiding her, and that would be just plain silly, wouldn't it? Please, come and join us. There's space at our table, and Jacinta would love to see you," Alice-Miranda coaxed.

"Well, I'll come and say hello, but really, I'm sure

I'm supposed to be somewhere else." Ambrosia fluttered her eyelashes and tilted her head ever so slightly toward Chef Vladimir.

"Pff, I'll see you later, darlink," Vladimir purred at Ambrosia.

"Do you know each other?" Alice-Miranda asked.

"Yes, of course. Vladimir runs a gorgeous restaurant in Moscow. Michelin stars and that sort of thing. I flew up there last week with some friends, and he tells me they're now booked solid for six months. The rotten paps from *Gloss and Goss* wouldn't leave us alone." Ambrosia looked smug. "But it was all for a good cause."

Alice-Miranda frowned. She didn't like to hear Mrs. Headlington-Bear talking about the paparazzi. They were the last thing Aunt Charlotte and Uncle Lawrence needed this week. At least everyone on board had signed a confidentiality agreement not to disclose any details before or after the wedding. And all inbound and outbound telephone calls were being monitored too. Aunty Gee's security wasn't taking any risks.

Ambrosia Headlington-Bear spent another few seconds surveying the party.

"I can't believe I don't recognize anyone," she said, barely masking her disappointment. "Oh, except the

Queen, of course—and that dishy Lawrence Ridley. I thought there'd be movie stars by the boatload."

"Aunt Charlotte and Uncle Lawrence were keen to keep it a mostly family affair," Alice-Miranda replied. "Is Mr. Headlington-Bear joining you for dinner?"

Ambrosia stared vacantly at the crowd, apparently lost in her own thoughts. "No," she replied absently.

"Well, please, come and sit with us," Alice-Miranda urged.

Ambrosia followed the tiny child, her kaftan swishing and flouncing. She was the sort of woman people couldn't help noticing.

Jacinta had been concentrating so hard on her dinner she'd almost hoovered up the entire contents of her plate.

Ambrosia glided over and stood behind her daughter. "Hello, Jacinta, this is a surprise. Have you got a kiss for Mummy?"

Jacinta swallowed her last mouthful. She wiped her hands on her napkin, stood up and turned around to greet her mother.

"I see you've still got a good appetite, darling." Ambrosia glanced at the empty plate. "Mind the grease on Mummy's new dress."

Jacinta gave Ambrosia an awkward hug. Her lips barely grazed her mother's cheek.

"Your mother hadn't realized that you were here," Alice-Miranda explained.

"Of course not." Jacinta frowned. "Why would anyone important invite me to anything interesting?"

The atmosphere around the table heaved under the weight of unspoken words.

"Hello, Mrs. Headlington-Bear," Millie said. "I'm Millie—it's good to finally meet you."

"Oh, hello. And for goodness' sake, call me Ambrosia. Mrs. Headlington-Bear sounds positively antique."

Ambrosia browsed around the table before her eyes came to rest on Lucas. She studied him carefully. "And who are you, young man?"

"I'm Lucas Nixon." He stood up and offered his hand. Lucas stared at her with his piercing black eyes and then smiled his million-dollar grin.

"And who do you belong to, Lucas?" she asked.

"My father is Lawrence Ridley," he replied.

"Well, that makes sense. It's no wonder you're so gorgeous, then, is it? Jacinta—make sure you keep an eye on this fellow."

Jacinta wished at that moment for a giant trapdoor to open up and swallow her mother whole.

Millie sniggered. "It's all right, Ambrosia. I think Jacinta's already got that under control."

A spurt of bile rose into the back of Jacinta's throat. "Thanks, Millie," she hissed.

"And who are you?" Ambrosia had turned her attention to Sep.

"Sep Sykes," he replied, standing and offering his hand as Lucas had done.

"Well, hello, Sep Sykes." Ambrosia's eyes sparkled. "Glad to see my daughter has such good taste in young men."

"Please, sit down, Ambrosia," Alice-Miranda invited her.

"No, I'm sure I'm supposed to be somewhere else." Ambrosia glanced around the deck.

An awkward silence descended over the table.

"Where's Daddy?" Jacinta asked.

"Oh, you know your father; it's all work, work, work. Excuse me." Ambrosia tapped a waiter on the shoulder. "Can you tell me where I'm meant to be sitting?"

"I won't be a moment, ma'am." The man scuttled off toward the maître d'.

"That's a lovely dress, Ambrosia," Alice-Miranda commented.

"Yes, it is, isn't it? I couldn't decide what to wear tonight. It took me ages to get ready. I mean, it was a bit stingy of the hosts not letting me bring Henri or Tiffany with me. I usually don't travel anywhere without them." Ambrosia inspected her manicured left hand as she spoke.

"Who are they?" Lucas asked.

"Henri's my stylist and he's a total saint, and Tiff does my hair and makeup. I must look a complete mess. It's the first time I've had to manage my own look in years," Ambrosia complained.

"Well, I think you look very pretty," Alice-Miranda complimented her.

"Yes, lovely," Millie added, elbowing Jacinta in the ribs.

"You look fine, Mummy," Jacinta muttered.

"Why don't I take a photograph of you and Jacinta?" Millie offered. She picked up her camera from the center of the table.

"Oh, of course." Ambrosia's smile lit up the deck. She leaned in beside her daughter, cheek to cheek.

Millie snapped three shots.

"Let me see," Ambrosia demanded as Millie reviewed the pictures. "Oh, that's gorgeous," Ambrosia remarked. "We look like sisters, Jacinta."

"Of course we do, Mother." Jacinta stared off into the distance, ignoring Millie and her camera.

The waiter returned. "Mrs. Headlington-Bear, if you'd like to follow me," he offered.

"See you later, children." Ambrosia pranced off to be seated with Max and Cyril, the Highton-Smith-Kennington-Joneses' stable hand and pilot.

Jacinta wrinkled her nose.

"I can't believe she didn't know I was here," she finally said. "How else did she think she got invited?"

"Don't be cross, Jacinta." Alice-Miranda put her hand on her friend's shoulder. "At least she knows you're here now, and you can spend some time together tomorrow."

"I doubt it," Jacinta snarled.

Alice-Miranda didn't reply. She had a niggling feeling in the bottom of her stomach, and right now she had no idea what to do about it.

After the main course, Dr. Lush appeared, dressed in his officer's uniform. He proceeded to make his way around the deck, swanning from one table to the next, apparently attempting to charm every woman on board. He introduced himself to Ambrosia Headlington-Bear, who seemed delighted by the attention. He had been rather glad to remove himself from an obnoxious old biddy called Albertine, who had been making overtures about his having tea tomorrow with her granddaughter, Daisy. She was a pretty young thing, for sure, but when the old woman told him they were in domestic service he had quickly withdrawn his charm. He had no desire to take up with the hired help—no matter how attractive they might be. And with heiresses from the bow to the stern, Nicholas couldn't help thinking he had landed in a sea of opportunity.

Alice-Miranda watched as he moved from table to table, laughing and smiling. With his dark eyes and prominent nose, she couldn't help thinking that he rather reminded her of someone else she'd met recently. She just couldn't work out who it was.

Chapter 14

Over at Aunty Gee's table, conversations had ranged from Mrs. Oliver's latest organic vegetable project to Lawrence's upcoming film and Alice-Miranda's school play. Between hoots of laughter and hushed whispers, there was barely a second's silence.

"Nasty business, those jewel heists," Hugh Kennington-Jones commented to Aunty Gee over his perfectly marinated lamb fillet. "It sounds like they're ticking off a very long list, if you ask me."

"Mmm." Aunty Gee nodded and swallowed. "I was chatting with Inspector Gerard just last week, and he assured me they're only after Russian gems. It's fortunate we haven't acquired any in our collection."

A spate of jewel thefts around the world over the past eighteen months had been a source of chronic irritation for Chief Inspector Sexton Gerard, the Head of Interpol. The common thread seemed to be the jewels' original owners, the long-departed Russian royal family. To date, all manner of trinkets had been stolen from private individuals on the Continent, museums in the United States and, most daringly, from the vault of the Kremlin in Moscow itself. Whoever was behind the raids was terribly well connected and exceedingly clever. So far, Gerard had no leads whatsoever.

"What's that, Aunty Gee?" Cecelia joined the conversation. "Has there been a robbery?"

"I was just saying, dear, that I don't think we have to worry at all about those nasty thieves who seem to be amassing a trove of Russian antiquities."

Having finished her meal, Alice-Miranda, with Millie in tow, hurried over to ask her parents if the children might be excused to play a game of hide-and-seek. She poked her head around next to her father and waited for him to finish speaking.

"I've heard they have the Great Imperial Crown

and the Scepter with the Orlov Diamond," Hugh said thoughtfully. "She's a real beauty that one—one of the largest in the world."

"Good heavens!" exclaimed Aunty Gee. "I would have thought the security at the Treasures of the Diamond Fund would have been better than that."

"What are you talking about?" Millie asked as she and Alice-Miranda squeezed in between Hugh's and Cecelia's chairs.

"Oh, hello, girls. We were just talking about some robberies of Russian jewels this past year or so," Hugh informed them.

"Why did you say *she's* a real beauty?" Alice-Miranda asked. "Is the diamond a girl?"

"I suppose I always think of jewels as being female," her father replied.

Alice-Miranda nodded. "May we be excused so we can play hide-and-seek?" She could see Jacinta and the boys at their table beckoning her and Millie to return.

"Of course, darling. Run along—but just stay above deck. Don't want anyone getting lost in the dark, do we?" Hugh directed.

Alice-Miranda pecked her father's cheek and then turned to give her mother the same treatment.

Millie waved. "Bye, everyone. Enjoy your dinner."

The group bid the girls farewell and went back to their conversations.

Deep in thought, Charlotte glanced up from her pork loin. "What about the Fabergé eggs?"

Queen Georgiana placed her knife and fork gently beside each other and drew her napkin to her lips. With furrowed brow, she folded her napkin and placed it beside her plate.

"Oh, my dear, I hadn't even given them a thought. Well, of course, they're more Russian than borscht, aren't they? I'll talk with Admiral Harding and Dalton. I know the security codes for the cabinets are a very well guarded secret, and I don't suppose it's especially common knowledge that they're on board."

"Gee, I think you're wrong there, dear," Granny Valentina piped up. "Don't you remember there was a feature on the *Octavia* in a recent edition of *Monarch Monthly*? I recall a lovely photograph of the drawing room with the cabinet in the background and at least a paragraph devoted to the eggs and how you happened to have them."

Aunty Gee's lips formed a perfect O. She signaled for Dalton to step forward from where he was standing behind her left shoulder.

A short conversation in hushed tones seemed to lighten her mood considerably.

"It's all right, dears." Aunty Gee giggled like a schoolgirl. She leaned in and motioned for the group to join her. "No need to worry at all," she whispered. "They're fakes."

"What do you mean, fakes?" Lawrence murmured, raising his eyebrows.

"Well, Dalton assures me that years ago my dear father had replicas made for the ship. He thought the *Octavia* was far too vulnerable. So the real eggs are in the vault at the palace. I can't imagine why no one has ever bothered to tell me, but perhaps that's because I never bothered to ask."

"Well, that's good news. Very good news indeed." Hugh nodded.

"Anyway, there's no need to worry. Dalton has the security well in hand." Aunty Gee smiled broadly.

Chapter 15

As the evening wore on, Neville Nordstrom felt decidedly bored. With no computer to distract him, time passed very slowly. There wasn't even a television in his room. He'd checked everywhere, thinking that perhaps it was well concealed in an antique piece of furniture or a recess in the floor or something, but no amount of searching had revealed any form of technology.

Henderson had appeared with a delicious plate of lamb loin chops, fillet steak, baked potatoes and an array of salads, exactly as he said he would. Neville's response to his questions consisted of nods or shakes of the head.

Neville currently didn't have any friends on dry land—well, none that he hadn't imagined—so he couldn't imagine he'd have any more luck making them at sea.

But the longer Neville spent with his own thoughts, the more diabolical they became. He pictured his father and mother arguing over whose fault it was that their one and only offspring was such an oddball. His father, a soccer-mad owner of a large earthmoving company, would never understand Neville's fascination for the natural world. Especially seeing as he made a living out of bulldozing it. His mother just wanted him to fit in. She was forever asking about his friends and who he sat with at school and who he talked to on the bus. He knew it made her anxious when he told her the truth, so he'd learned to make things up. It was easier that way. It hadn't always been like this. Back at home he had friends. It was just that being shy and not speaking the language made it twice as hard to meet people, and Neville found the whole process exhausting.

Just before nine p.m. Neville made the decision to leave the relative safety of his cabin and seek some air on the decks above. With his trumpet case in hand, he walked the twenty or so steps along the corridor to the stairway. Ascending two flights of stairs, he found himself at the end of a long deck. There was quite a commotion coming from above, and he was keen to steer clear of the crowd. Neville gazed out to sea while edging his way slowly along the starboard side of the ship. The ocean was calm, like a sheet of glass, and there couldn't have been any swell. In fact, if he hadn't known they were steaming for New York, Neville might have been fooled into thinking that the ship was not moving at all.

He walked as far as he could without having to ascend to the busy deck above. There was music playing—the type his father liked to listen to on a Saturday afternoon following a particularly successful game of soccer. Neville glanced up and saw that there were people dancing. There were women in colorful frocks and men in smart suits calling out and laughing as if they had all known each other for twenty years. Neville was too anxious to socialize during the journey. He just wanted to fulfill his mission—and work out how he would get his parents to forgive him.

He had to stick to his plan. Once he'd completed his trek from New York and explained himself, surely his friend would understand. More than that, with

Neville there in person, he'd have to help. The two of them would be hailed as heroes (he wasn't looking forward to that part) and written up in *Scientific Scientist* magazine (that would be okay, as long as he didn't have to talk to anyone too much).

Neville was lost in his thoughts when suddenly, from the corner of his eye, he spotted the girl from the hallway crouched down behind a lifeboat. She was staring straight toward him.

"Shh." She raised her finger to her lips. "I'm hiding. Please don't tell them I'm here."

Neville really hadn't wanted to talk to her when he met her earlier, and he especially didn't want to talk to her now.

"Come here." She waved her right hand. "If you hide too, then you won't give me away."

Neville sniffed. He would rather have fled back to his cabin. There was a shuffling sound on the deck above and a boy's voice.

"I saw something—over there—come on, Sep!" the boy shouted. "I think Alice-Miranda's up near the pool!"

The two lads raced away, and Neville, who had held his breath, let out a shallow sigh.

"Come on," Alice-Miranda whispered again. "They'll be back soon."

Neville clutched his case to his chest and made a dash across the open deck. He ducked in beside the girl.

"Hello, Neville." Alice-Miranda smiled at him. "I thought it was you. I recognized your case."

Neville gripped it tighter.

"You must be very dedicated to your instrument," Alice-Miranda commented.

Neville didn't know what to say.

"Isn't this the most delicious party ever?" she asked. "Would you like to join our game? We're playing hide-and-seek, and I think I might make a run for it back to base in a minute. You can come too, if you want."

Neville shook his head.

Alice-Miranda had a strange feeling about young Neville and his case. There was something that just didn't feel right, but now was not the time to investigate.

"Oh, all right then, perhaps I'll see you later." And with that Alice-Miranda stood up and sped along the open deck, up the nearest flight of steps and toward the stanchion the children had decided would be home.

A sound like gunfire punctured the still night air and a starburst of silver rained from the sky, then another and another. Neville jumped like a startled cat. He promptly decided that he'd had enough fresh air and scurried back down to his cabin, where he changed into his pajamas, dived into his freshly turned-down bed and fell asleep reading the latest edition of *Scientific Scientist*.

Chapter 16

Alice-Miranda and her friends had fallen into bed late that night after the delicious barbecue dinner followed by their energetic game of hide-and-seek. Poppy and Annie were feeling a little better, and they and almost all of Alice-Miranda's distant cousins had joined the group. They had even coaxed Shilly and Max to play too, until the game was interrupted by the spectacular fireworks display.

In their suite the next morning, the girls were just beginning to stir.

"Wasn't last night wonderful?" Alice-Miranda yawned and stretched her arms out behind her before sitting up in her bed.

"Good morning." Millie rubbed her eyes and rolled over to face her friend. "Are you awake, Jacinta?" Millie asked.

But Jacinta's bed was empty.

"I wonder where she's gone?" Alice-Miranda asked. "I hope she's all right."

There was a sharp rap at the bedroom door. It opened and Winterstone appeared. "Good morning, young ladies."

"Hello, Mr. Winterstone," said Alice-Miranda. "How are you today?"

Unaccustomed to being asked about his welfare, Winterstone was momentarily lost for words. In his job, it was usually he who did all the asking.

"I am as well as can be expected for a man of my age and station," he replied thoughtfully.

"Well, that's good to hear," said Alice-Miranda.

Winterstone drew back the heavy curtains to reveal sunlight dancing on a pondlike ocean, scattering diamonds on the azure water.

"Oh, what a glorious day!" Alice-Miranda leapt from her bed to take a closer look. Their cabin on the port side of the ship offered an excellent vista.

"Have you seen Jacinta?" Millie asked Winterstone.

"Yes, miss, she passed me in the hallway and mentioned something about going for a run around the deck. Strangely, she didn't feel the need to comment on my hair this morning," he said, raising his left eyebrow at Millie.

"Oh, that's good." Millie pushed back the covers and walked over to join Alice-Miranda by the window.

"Do you know where we are, Mr. Winterstone?" Alice-Miranda asked.

"Yes, I believe we are anchored off Nice. That's the city over there beyond the beach."

"It's so pretty!" Alice-Miranda stared at the view. A long stretch of white sand joined the ocean to the shoreline with the buildings rising behind.

While the girls admired the scene outside, Winterstone opened the wardrobe and selected three outfits, laying one carefully on each girl's bed. "Would you like to have breakfast in your suite or would you prefer to join your parents upstairs in the Breakfast Room?"

"I think we should go and see everyone upstairs." Alice-Miranda spun around. "Oh, Mr. Winterstone, you don't have to get our clothes ready for us." Alice-Miranda picked up her pants and top and held them against herself. "But you do have a lovely eye for putting things together. I've never thought of wearing this green top with these pants, but they look good, don't they, Millie?"

Millie glanced over at her. "Yes, they do, actually," she replied. "I'm going to have a shower."

Winterstone retreated to the sitting room, where he set about pouring three large tumblers of orange juice from a jug on the sideboard.

Alice-Miranda followed him into the room.

"I took the liberty of arranging some fresh juice for you, miss. I thought you might be thirsty." At which point he flicked the retractable ruler from his jacket pocket and measured three spots on the coffee table before carefully placing each glass just so.

"Gosh, you are precise, Mr. Winterstone," Alice-Miranda complimented him. "When we have banquets at home, Mrs. Shillingsworth gets her tape measure out and makes sure that every setting is exactly the same, but that's only when we have loads of guests. Usually it's much more haphazard. Especially when I'm given the job of setting the table."

"It's my training, miss." He covered the leftover juice in the carafe with a dainty net cloth.

"Do you have a family, Mr. Winterstone?" Alice-Miranda asked.

Again, unaccustomed to being asked anything much, Winterstone hesitated. What was it about

this tiny child with her huge brown eyes? Winterstone wondered.

Alice-Miranda noticed his discomfort. "I'm sorry.
I know I ask too many questions. Anyway, I think
Millie is out of the shower, so I'll run along and get
ready. Thank you for the juice." She smiled.

Chapter 17

Neville Nordstrom could not remember the last time he'd enjoyed such a good sleep. The gentle motion of the ship had sent him off almost as soon as his head hit the pillow. His mind was filled with dreams, which had fractured into a thousand tiny pieces as soon as he woke up—but he felt warm inside, like after a hot chocolate on a frosty day.

"Good morning, Master Neville." Henderson knocked and opened the bedroom door. Neville clutched the covers and drew them to his chin.

"Would you like something to drink? Perhaps a glass of juice?" the steward asked.

Neville barely moved his head. He seemed to have the uncanny ability of shaking his eyes up and down.

"Very good, sir. I'll leave you to get dressed, then." Henderson retreated from the room and set about preparing a tray with some juice and a shiny apple.

He was trying hard not to judge, but the boy was quite the strangest lad he'd ever encountered. And what was his obsession with that trumpet case? Henderson had to stop himself from laughing out loud when he noticed its outline under the covers at the bottom of the bed.

Inside the bedroom Neville waited a couple of minutes before he pushed back the duvet and hopped out of bed. He walked across the room and peered through one of the portholes. From his cabin on the starboard side of the ship all he could see was miles and miles of endless ocean. He wondered for a moment what would happen if the ship struck an iceberg. Like the *Titanic*. He supposed that they would all die an icy death in the subzero temperatures of the Atlantic.

Dismissing the thought from his mind, Neville pulled his backpack from the bottom of the wardrobe, opened it up and located a clean pair of underpants and his favorite yellow polo shirt. He'd caught

Henderson trying to unpack his bag and managed to find enough voice to object. He wanted to have everything in one place in case he needed to leave the ship in a hurry—like in the event of an iceberg or something.

The lad pulled on his beige trousers and sat down to put on his shoes and socks. He stared at his grubby trainers. Neville's mother had suggested they go and buy a new pair last week, but he'd told her not to worry. Now he rather wished he hadn't put her off. In the opulence of his cabin, they looked especially shabby.

He emerged from his bedroom hoping that Henderson would have left him some juice and gone away. But he hadn't. Neville stood clutching his case in the doorway.

"Will you be dining with your mother in the Breakfast Room this morning, sir?" Henderson asked, holding back a grin.

Neville shook his head. He wondered why Henderson mentioned his mother. She certainly wasn't here.

"Very well, Master Neville. Would you like me to bring you some breakfast, then?" Henderson was starting to wonder if there was really something amiss with this unfortunate kid.

Neville moved his head ever so slightly. Henderson withdrew from the cabin and Neville sat down to look at the newspaper on the coffee table.

On page three Neville was surprised to see a face he recognized smiling out at him. He checked the name and wondered what the article was about. He wished he'd paid more attention in his Spanish language classes—there were only a few words here and there that he understood.

Neville checked the date on the paper. The pages didn't feel like newsprint. And he wondered how they would get the paper out here in the middle of the ocean anyway.

Neville thumbed through the rest of the paper, picking up the odd word here and there before flipping back to page three.

Henderson returned with a breakfast tray laden with pancakes and maple syrup, bacon and eggs, several boxes of cereal, milk, fruit salad and more juice.

"I hope everything will be to your liking, Master Neville." The steward sat the tray down on the small table for two which stood in an alcove at the end of the sitting room.

Neville sat at the table and glanced warily at the steward. Henderson decided that Neville might be more comfortable attending to his own breakfast, so he moved over to the couch and began to plump the cushions. It was then that he noticed the newspaper on the coffee table.

"I am sorry, sir; I've given you the Spanish newspaper. We have them printed from the Internet, and I must have picked that up by mistake. He's a busy man." Henderson pointed at the photograph.

"Wh-wh-what does it say?" Neville whispered.

"Oh, he's heading to Spain," Henderson replied.

"Wh-wh-when?" Neville stammered.

"I think he's there tomorrow. A two-week tour—very unexpected—some business and then a holiday by the sea, it says."

Neville gulped. His eyes spun and his brain felt like it was packed tightly with cotton wool. Without warning he slumped forward and his head glanced off the corner of the cereal bowl and hit the table with a thud. A trickle of blood began to ooze from his eyebrow.

"Are you all right, Master Neville?" Henderson rushed to his side. But the poor boy was out cold.

Chapter 18

Alice-Miranda and Millie were seated with Millie's parents, her grandfather Ambrose and Mrs. Oliver for breakfast. Hugh and Cecelia were yet to appear. Charlotte and Lawrence were holding court at a long table with over twenty of their friends vying for the happy couple's attention.

Alice-Miranda had given them a wave when she and Millie had entered the room. She would catch up with them later when they weren't quite so busy. Except that Alice-Miranda hadn't yet found an occasion when they weren't being mobbed by guests.

Alice-Miranda waved to Poppy and Annie, who

were sitting at an adjacent table. Their mother, Lady Sarah, was still looking a little off-color.

"Gosh, your mother's cousin wears a lot of jewelry," Millie commented.

"Mummy says Lady Sarah has one of the best collections in the world," Alice-Miranda replied.

"Those diamond earrings are enormous. I wonder if she'll let me take a photo of her." Millie picked her camera up from the table.

"I'm sure that the guests don't need to be stalked by you and your camera, Millicent," her father tutted. "Please put it away for a while."

"But, Dad, those earrings are the size of Ping-Pong balls—no one will believe me if I don't—" Millie began.

Hamish was firm. "And Lady Sarah can wear earrings the size of bowling balls if she chooses—and she doesn't need you pestering her for a picture. You are not the ship's own paparazzo."

"Oh, I didn't think of it like that," Millie replied.

Alice-Miranda giggled.

"Imagine earrings the size of bowling balls. That would be like having three heads." Millie chuckled.

Four waiters arrived and simultaneously deposited all manner of tasty treats in front of the hungry diners.

"These look rather good," Ambrose McLoughlin-

McTavish commented as he dug his fork into the mountain of scrambled eggs on his plate.

"Yes, I must agree," Mrs. Oliver said.

"Really?" Alice-Miranda stared at Dolly Oliver across the table.

"And why ever do you say that, young lady?" Several rows of lines puckered on Mrs. Oliver's forehead.

"Because you hate having other people cook for you. Whenever we've been away before, you nearly always commandeer the kitchen by the second day," Alice-Miranda informed the group. "I'm surprised you're not downstairs."

There really wasn't anything Dolly Oliver didn't know about cooking. She'd been the Highton-Smith-Kennington-Joneses' family cook for the past ten years and with the Highton-Smiths for another thirty years before that. Dolly was renowned for her amazing food and her incredible scientific work too. Her product, Just Add Water Freeze-Dried Foods, was being shipped around the world, making important inroads into malnutrition. But just recently, since Dolly had been reacquainted with Millie's grandfather, Alice-Miranda had noticed a change in her. Almost as though, for the first time in her life, she was happy letting other people look after her—well just a little bit, anyway.

"That's not entirely true, young lady." Mrs. Oliver looked over at Alice-Miranda. "I didn't go near Prince Shivaji's chef, Amir, when we were in Jaipur last year," she said.

"Well, that's only because he insisted on keeping a basket of spitting cobras beside the stove," Alice-Miranda reminded her. "I wasn't going anywhere near that kitchen either."

Mrs. Oliver snorted and turned to the rest of the table. "Oh dear, I do remember that. Amir's father was a snake charmer, and he often had his son mind his serpents overnight. I was having a tour of the kitchen, wanting to learn all about the wonderful spices he was using, when I got a little bit nosy and lifted the lid on the basket. You can only imagine my reaction when a full-grown cobra reared up and looked me in the eye."

Everyone laughed at the thought of poor Mrs. Oliver and the snake.

"Well, I dare you to try and get a job in the kitchen on the *Octavia,* Mrs. Oliver," Millie challenged.

"Why do you say that, dear?" the old woman quizzed.

"We met the head chef, Vladimir, yesterday and he's fierce. His men are terrified of him," Millie reported.

"What a pity," Mrs. Oliver replied. "I so enjoyed

that marinated lamb we had last night. I was planning to pop in and ask if he might share the recipe."

"Well, good luck," Millie offered.

Jacinta appeared at the entrance to the room.

"Would you like to sit with your mother and father this morning, miss?" a young crewman offered.

"Are they here?" Jacinta looked perplexed. It wasn't at all like her mother to be out of bed before noon, let alone up and eating breakfast at the ungodly hour of eight a.m.

"Over there, miss." The young man pointed toward Hugh and Cecelia, who had slipped into the breakfast room a few minutes beforehand.

"Oh, they're not my parents." Jacinta felt a sharp stab deep inside her stomach.

"I am terribly sorry, miss," the crewman replied, his cheeks turning red.

"Yeah, me too," Jacinta whispered. "It's all right, I'll sit with my friends." She looked toward the adjacent table, where Alice-Miranda was holding court.

Chapter 19

Neville's eyes opened and he wondered for a moment where he was.

"Are you all right, Master Neville?" Henderson leaned over the boy, who was lying on his back on the king-sized bed in his suite. "I've called for the doctor."

Neville sat up. His gaze darted around the room, like a mosquito in search of a bare limb, before he realized that his case was in fact sitting on the bed beside him.

"I know you're awfully attached to that instrument, sir, so I brought it back in for you."

Neville swallowed hard and managed to mumble a soft thank-you.

"You're welcome. Now, how are you feeling?"

Neville rubbed his forehead and wondered why there was a towel wrapped around his head. He couldn't for the life of him remember what had happened.

"We were just talking about J. Gatsby Grayson and then the next thing I knew you were facedown in your cereal. It was lucky I was here or you might have drowned," Henderson went on, exaggerating somewhat, as Neville's head had actually come to rest on the table.

At the mention of the name, the painful memory started flooding back. Neville couldn't believe it. How dare he leave the United States and travel all the way to Spain, of all places, just as Neville was leaving Spain, on a ship, risking his life to visit him and explain his amazing discovery?

Henderson interrupted the boy's thoughts. "You're looking awfully pale, Master Neville. Would you like a sip of water?"

There was a loud rap at the cabin door and Henderson left the bedroom to answer it.

"Well, what is it?" Dr. Nicholas Lush asked as he followed Henderson into the sitting room.

"I think he fainted. His head hit the side of the cereal bowl. Did some damage too. He chipped the bowl, and I think there might be a small piece of Her Majesty's china embedded above his right eye. There was quite a deal of blood, but I wrapped a towel around his head and laid him on his bed. He's just come around now," Henderson explained to the doctor.

"I suppose I should have a look at him." Dr. Lush walked through into Neville's bedroom. He glanced at Neville, picked up the boy's wrist and then studied his watch. "So, you fainted, did you?"

Neville didn't know what to say, so he said nothing.

"Well, how do you feel now?" Dr. Lush asked. He placed Neville's arm back down beside him.

"O-o-okay," Neville stammered.

"Get that grubby thing off the bed," the doctor snapped, pointing at Neville's case.

Neville found his voice. "NO!" He reached out and pulled it in close and then pushed it under the covers beside him.

"What's in it?" Nicholas Lush sneered. "A golden trumpet?"

Neville glared.

Dr. Lush leaned forward and unwrapped the towel from around Neville's forehead. "Ah, yes, there does seem to be a piece of the Queen's china lodged just above your eye, young man. I think that will require some digging and then a stitch or two. I suppose we'd better have you taken up to the infirmary, where I keep my weapons." Lush raised his eyebrows.

"Weapons?" Neville rasped, and started to shake. Henderson came to his rescue.

"May I have a word, sir?" Henderson indicated the other room.

"Make it snappy. This has thrown my whole day out." Dr. Lush followed the younger man into the sitting room. Henderson closed the bedroom door.

"Doctor, I think Neville would prefer to stay here, if he might. I can keep an eye on him while you get whatever you need," the steward suggested. "He's just about the shyest kid I've ever met in my life. He hardly ever says boo, and when he does manage to speak it's one word at a time. I think he might have a complete breakdown if you have to take him to the infirmary. If it's all the same to you and you can do the work down here, I promise I'll watch him."

Nicholas Lush didn't mind at all. He had loads to do—and attending to a slightly injured, noncommunicative boy with a paper-thin constitution was not on the list.

There was much more fun to be had on deck, talking with all those lovely ladies.

"Well, where are his parents?" Dr. Lush asked. "I

won't be doing anything until I have their permission. The boy will need local anesthetic and stitches."

Nicholas was painfully aware that Admiral Harding was quite the stickler for rules and regulations, and the last thing the good doctor wanted was any undue attention from the boss, who didn't seem to like him much at the best of times.

"His mother's just across the hallway."

"Well, go and get her, or at the very least have her sign this." Dr. Lush pulled a notepad from his bag, scrawled an illegible sentence and tore off the top page. "I'll wait with the boy until you get back, and then I'll have to get some more supplies from upstairs."

Henderson walked across the hallway and tapped loudly on Ambrosia Headlington-Bear's suite door. There was no answer, so he let himself in. The sitting room was swathed in darkness and the bedroom door was closed. He knocked gently.

"Yes?" a husky voice called from within.

"Good morning, ma'am." Henderson peeked inside.

"I need a coffee," Ambrosia mumbled.

"Very well, ma'am, but I need you to sign something." Henderson stepped into the room. Mrs. Headlington-Bear was lying under the covers, a sleeping mask shielding her eyes.

"What? Are they going to charge me for room service?" she snapped.

"No, ma'am, it's . . ."

"Don't talk. My head is throbbing," Ambrosia complained. "I've got a migraine."

"But, ma'am," Henderson tried again.

"Just give me the piece of paper and bring me some coffee." Ambrosia sat up. She pushed the mask over her head and grabbed the pen from Henderson. Without even looking, she scrawled a messy signature at the bottom of the page.

"But, Mrs. Headlington-Bear, you should know what you're signing . . . ," he began.

"Is it life-or-death?" Ambrosia drawled.

Henderson tried again. "Well, no, not exactly. But it's about your child."

"My child? My child does perfectly well without me." Ambrosia sank down into her pillows. She snapped the mask back over her eyes and pulled the covers above her head.

"Leave," Ambrosia snapped. "I need to sleep."

Henderson retreated from Mrs. Headlington-Bear's suite wondering what had just happened.

He walked back across the hallway to find the doctor drumming his fingers on the sideboard.

"Well, did you get it?" Dr. Lush demanded.

"Yes, but I don't think she's in the running for any Mother of the Year awards," Henderson said with a frown.

"Not my problem." Dr. Lush pushed the piece of paper into his top pocket. "I'll be back shortly. But someone has to watch the boy for the next few hours," he informed Henderson.

"That's all right. I've only got him to look after, and his mother, and I know that she's got an extended booking at the spa this afternoon, as I made the appointment myself."

"Very well then. I'll get my bag." Dr. Lush headed off.

Half an hour later, Neville was sporting two stitches, a blackening eye and a bump on his forehead. Henderson, who was taking his duties very seriously, had made himself at home on the sofa next to Neville's bed. Fortunately, the doctor had given the boy some rather strong pain medication, and he had quickly fallen fast asleep.

"So what's so special about that trumpet of yours?" Henderson smiled to himself as he observed the tatty case perched beside his young charge. He'd been wondering about it ever since Neville had arrived on the ship and shown the old thing such undying devotion.

He might even have risked opening it and taking a peek, but not at that moment. He didn't want to be in any more trouble with the first officer.

The steward walked back into the sitting room and ran his eyes along the bookshelves, looking for something that might keep him awake for the next few hours.

"The Great Gatsby." Henderson pulled the book out. "Okay, Mr. F. Scott Fitzgerald, what's all this about?"

Chapter 20

Alice-Miranda, Millie and Jacinta finished their breakfast and, together with Lucas and Sep, who'd arrived a little while after the girls, planned the day ahead. They decided to spend the morning at the pool, followed by some games on deck and maybe a movie in the small theater during the afternoon. Admiral Harding had announced at breakfast that there was the strong possibility of a storm that evening, and given some recent weather activity in the region, he predicted that the passengers might be confined to their cabins if a gale blew up.

"Well, come on, we'd best make the most of the

day," Alice-Miranda instructed. She stopped to greet her parents on the way out of the breakfast room but still couldn't get near her aunt or Lawrence, who seemed to have a never-ending queue of well-wishers demanding their attention.

The children hurried off to change into their bathers and met back on the glass-covered pool deck. The deck chairs were filling fast, as the guests were making the most of the unseasonally warm sunshine.

Alice-Miranda and Sep laid their towels out on adjacent recliners and sat down.

Sep glanced around at the rows of glamorous women in their brightly colored swimsuits. "My mother would have loved this," he remarked.

"How is she?" Alice-Miranda asked.

"Oh, fine, I think. She and Dad adore Spain, and I'm assuming my mother spends all day every day lying by the pool at their villa anyway," he replied. "It's funny, but I do miss them a little."

"Of course you do. That's perfectly understandable," Alice-Miranda replied. "Have you talked to your sister at all?"

"No, not really. Whenever I call, she just hands the phone straight to Mum or Dad."

"I've written her a few letters," Alice-Miranda offered. "I hope she's received them."

"Really? I mean, after what Mum and Sloane did? It was pretty unforgivable," Sep concluded.

"They just got carried away, that's all. There's always a reason why people behave the way they do. You can't really blame Sloane—she was just doing what your mother asked her to—and it's hard to say no to grown-ups," Alice-Miranda replied.

"I'm sure you don't find it hard to say no—to anyone." Sep smiled.

"Well, if you're talking to Sloane at all, please tell her that I'd love to hear some news," said Alice-Miranda. "In fact, I think I might write to her this afternoon." And with that she skipped over to the side of the pool and jumped into its crystal depths.

Sep grinned to himself. He'd really never met anyone like Alice-Miranda.

The children spent so long in the water that by the time they hopped out, their fingertips and toes were shriveled like raisins.

"I'm starving," Millie complained. "We should go and get some lunch."

"Last one to the dining room's a rotten egg," Lucas challenged.

The children raced across the deck toward their

towels when Alice-Miranda felt a stabbing pain in her left foot.

"Ow!" She winced.

"What's the matter?" Jacinta asked.

Alice-Miranda hopped over to the sun lounge to inspect the damage, leaving a trail of red spots behind her.

Millie and Jacinta rushed over to her.

"It feels like there's something in my foot," said Alice-Miranda, flinching as she held it up for her friends to examine. Small drops of blood leaked onto the deck.

"I'd say you've got a splinter." Millie pulled Alice-Miranda's leg up to take a closer look. A shard of timber was poking out from the soft flesh between her toes.

"That's not a splinter," Jacinta remarked. "More like a miniature javelin or a giant's toothpick."

Millie glared at Jacinta. She didn't want to alarm Alice-Miranda, but it did seem a little more serious than a splinter, and Jacinta wasn't helping at all.

"We'll have to tell Admiral Harding," Jacinta proclaimed. "That's really not good for a royal yacht."

Millie and Alice-Miranda exchanged quizzical glances.

"Splinters. You shouldn't be getting splinters off

the deck of the *Octavia*," Jacinta tutted. "You'd think they'd have better maintenance, and the ship's just been renovated."

Lucas peered at Alice-Miranda's foot, which was now streaked with red.

"You'll have to get it out," he offered. "Or it might turn septic."

"And then you'll have to get your leg amputated like my granny's friend Ossie," Jacinta added.

"That's terrible!" Alice-Miranda gasped. "Did he have a splinter?"

"No, he had gangrene from years of heavy smoking, but his leg turned septic and they had to cut it off anyway."

"Jacinta!" the children chorused. Millie gave her a shove.

"You'll need to see the doctor," Millie advised as she grabbed a towel and tried to mop up some of the blood.

The children glanced around the deck. It seemed that all of the adults had already headed off to lunch.

Alice-Miranda stood up. She couldn't put pressure on the front of her foot at all, so with Lucas on one arm and Millie on the other, she hopped inside.

"We'll come too," Jacinta offered.

"No, why don't you and Sep go and organize something to eat? We won't be long," Alice-Miranda called.

"Are you sure?" Jacinta replied. "You might have to have horrible huge needles, and it could take a while to get that monster out."

"Jacinta!" Millie glared. "Just go and get some lunch."

Lucas looked at Alice-Miranda. "It won't be that bad."

"I'm sure Dr. Lush will be very gentle," Millie reassured her friend.

Chapter 21

The children arrived at the infirmary to find Dr. Lush outside taping a handwritten sign to the door.

"I'm so glad we caught you," Millie panted.

"What?" The doctor spun around to find Alice-Miranda flagged by her friends.

"Godfathers," Nicholas breathed. "What's the matter now?" He'd had enough of children already today.

"Alice-Miranda has a splinter and she needs you to get it out," Millie informed him.

"A splinter? For heaven's sake, couldn't one of you have dug it out? There's a first-aid kit on the pool deck, which is obviously where you've come from . . . dripping water all over my floor. And you do have parents, don't you?" He unlocked the door and walked back into the consulting room. "Well, are you coming?"

"Interesting bedside manner," Lucas whispered, catching Millie's attention. Millie rolled her eyes.

"I am so sorry to inconvenience you, Dr. Lush," Alice-Miranda began. "It's just that I was running and tripped on the deck and I seem to have acquired a rather *large* splinter in my foot."

Dr. Lush let out an exasperated sigh and instructed the children to help Alice-Miranda over to the examination table.

"Hop up there," he directed.

Alice-Miranda attempted to push herself up but caught her damaged foot on the stool.

"Ouch," she squeaked. "I think I might need some help."

Millie and Lucas glared at the doctor.

"What?" he said. "Oh, you want *me* to lift her up?" He curled his lip and huffed loudly before depositing Alice-Miranda on the table.

Nicholas Lush was not having a good day. Between that pasty boy in the Albert Suite and several nasty bouts of seasickness, which he couldn't understand given that the ocean resembled a millpond,

Nicholas's intention to spend his time making better acquaintance with some of the lovely ladies on board had not worked out at all. And now a splinter had put paid to his lunch plans.

He held up his right hand and with rather over-dramatic flair wrenched a latex glove over his out-stretched fingers, then repeated the act for his left. He fished around in the top drawer of his desk and found a magnifying glass with which to inspect the minuscule fragment.

He picked up Alice-Miranda's heel and moved her foot up toward the glass.

"Good Lord." He reeled in openmouthed horror. "That's not a splinter. You could whittle a figure-head from that beast." His heart began to thump, and he wondered what sort of surgery might be required to remove the shard protruding from between Alice-Miranda's toes.

Alice-Miranda bit her lip and looked to her friends for reassurance.

"Way to go, Dr. Lush," Lucas admonished. "I'm sure Alice-Miranda is feeling much better now."

"Find her parents," Dr. Lush commanded.

"Oh, it's all right," Alice-Miranda advised. "Millie can hold my hand, sir. I'll be fine."

"That's well and good, but you will be requiring an anesthetic and quite likely some stitches with the mess that will make . . . I mean the extent of the digging required, and I won't be doing anything until I have signed permission from one of your parents," Dr. Lush stated. "In the meantime, I suppose I can give you something mild for the pain." He looked at Alice-Miranda's foot and shuddered.

Alice-Miranda sat patiently on the examination table. Millie and Lucas had done as they were told and gone to locate her parents. Dr. Lush retreated to his desk, where he looked to be consulting a thick medical textbook.

"Have you removed many splinters like this one before?" Alice-Miranda asked.

"Of course," he snapped.

"Then may I ask, why are you looking in that book?" She craned her neck to get a better view.

"Nerves," he replied.

"Oh, don't be nervous," Alice-Miranda soothed. "I'm sure you'll do a perfectly good job."

"I'm not nervous, you silly child," he bit. "You have nerves in your foot. I just want to check that I'm not about to damage any of them."

"Oh," Alice-Miranda sighed. "That's a relief. Because I'd be a little bit nervous myself if you were anxious at all."

Lush was reading, midsentence and deep in thought, when the telephone rang. He hesitated, then picked up the receiver. "Lush," he answered. "Not now. I have a patient." He was clearly not enjoying the conversation. "What do you mean she's *missing*? We're on a ship—she can't be far," he breathed. "Well, find her, you imbecile!" The doctor slammed the telephone down.

"Is everything all right, Dr. Lush?" Alice-Miranda asked.

"Of course," he snapped. "Why wouldn't it be?"

"Well, it's just that you seemed a little bit cross on the telephone. I'm sure being a doctor on a ship must be a difficult job—people after you all hours of the day and night. What is it that you've lost—or should I say who?" she asked. "Perhaps I can help. Aunty Gee told us that we could have the run of the ship, so my friends and I had a really good look around yesterday, and I think we saw just about every part of it—well, except inside the suites, of course, because it would be terribly rude to go barging in on people's private areas. But other than that, we went everywhere; except the engine room too. So I'm sure that if you tell me who you're looking for, Millie and Jacinta and Lucas and Sep and I could try and find her for you."

"I don't know what you're talking about," Nicholas Lush scoffed. "I didn't say I'd lost anyone. I think the medicine must have made you a little bit silly, young lady."

Alice-Miranda frowned. She knew what she'd heard. Dr. Lush had just told someone on the telephone, who must also have been on the ship, that someone was lost. She wasn't affected by any medication at all.

"But, Dr. Lush, you didn't give me any medication," Alice-Miranda replied.

"Of course I did!" he barked. He turned around to see the container of paracetamol open on his desk and two small tablets sitting beside a full glass of water.

She was right. He hadn't given her any medication.

His face flushed red. "Well, you'd better have it now."

Nicholas wished he hadn't taken that call. Something told him that this tiny child, with her cascading chocolate curls and eyes as big as saucers, was a meddlesome little creature.

Alice-Miranda was getting one of her strange feelings.

The operation to remove Alice-Miranda's giant splinter took rather much longer than Nicholas Lush had hoped. He had other things on his mind but knew that if he messed this up his life wasn't worth living.

Her mother, the charming Cecelia Highton-Smith, had promptly arrived at the infirmary, horrified by the scene in front of her. Nicholas gave her something to soothe her nerves and reassured her that everything would be just fine. Then he gave the child a local anesthetic and spent what seemed like an age coaxing the timber from between her delicate toes. In the end there was hardly a mark—and no stitches required. It was the best work he'd done in quite a while. Cecelia Highton-Smith was so grateful that she invited the doctor to join her and her husband, Hugh, for dinner. Nicholas was thrilled. The Highton-Smith-Kennington-Joneses knew everyone who was anyone.

Chapter 22

When the pesky child and her lovely mother finally left the surgery, Nicholas got on the telephone quick-smart.

"So have you found her yet?" he growled into the receiver. Tiny beads of perspiration formed along his brow. "What was she in? Oh, for heaven's sake, was that the best you could do? Well, I can tell you that you'd better find her, and soon."

Nicholas Lush slammed the receiver down. He couldn't believe his ears. This was awful. He slumped down in his chair and leaned forward on his desk, his head cradled in his hands.

The telephone rang.

He reached out and snatched it up. "What now?" Nicholas was fuming. "It had better be good news. . . . Oh, I'm sorry, sir. Yes, yes, had a little bit of bad news earlier, but I'm sure things will be fine. You want to inspect the records this afternoon? Certainly, Admiral. Half an hour. Of course." Nicholas patted away the perspiration on his forehead.

He reached forward and wiggled the mouse to wake his computer. Fortunately he knew well Admiral Harding's love of spot inspections.

Nicholas was up to date with his records for the week—mostly doling out the odd headache tablet here and there to the crew, and of course, yesterday there was the horrendous seasickness he'd dealt with when guests had come aboard. Annoyingly, today's minor surgeries would take longer to record.

Nicholas's stomach gurgled and growled. He was eager to finish the pesky paperwork as quickly as possible, and then, hopefully, the admiral would arrive on time. He didn't want to miss afternoon canapés, having been forced to skip lunch.

Nicholas entered the name Alice-Miranda Highton-Smith-Kennington-Jones into the computer. Her suite name appeared, along with some other details about her age and parents. Nicholas typed his notes quickly.

Once he'd completed her record, he pulled the piece of paper containing the permission from the lad's mother from his top pocket. He'd forgotten to get the boy's full name from the steward.

Nicholas studied the handwriting. He could have sworn that it said A. Headlington-Bear. That was odd. She hadn't mentioned anything about a son when they'd been talking last evening. But then again, the woman was an appalling flirt, and perhaps she'd thought he'd pay her less attention if she mentioned a child. He wouldn't have.

Nicholas brought up a new entry. He tapped in the surname Headlington-Bear. Three names blinked on the screen in front of him. Ambrosia Headlington-Bear, Jacinta Headlington-Bear and Neville Headlington-Bear. He entered Neville's name into the report and began to type the details of the incident when he glanced at the patient's age. Apparently Master Neville was forty-eight years old. That was odd. The records were linked directly to the National Health database. He entered Ambrosia's name. That was interesting. She was forty-one. Certainly a surprise, given she didn't look a day over thirty. He entered Jacinta's name. Age eleven. This was very strange indeed.

So, if the boy wasn't, in fact, Neville Headlington-

Bear, then who on earth was he, and what was he doing in Mr. Headlington-Bear's suite? "Children," Nicholas murmured. "Can't be trusted, can they?"

The doctor sighed. He rested his elbows on the desk in front of him and exhaled through his clenched fist. Nicholas hit the delete button on the computer. Master Neville's surgery didn't need writing up at all. But the lad needed a house call.

Nicholas stood up. There was a sharp rap on the door. He really didn't have time for any more patients—there were other more important things on his mind.

"Lush!" a voice boomed from the hallway.

"Coming, sir." Nicholas opened the door to find Admiral Harding flagged by First Officer Prendergast.

"You're earlier than I expected, sir." Nicholas gulped.

"I hope everything is in order." The admiral glanced at his watch. By his calculations he was exactly on time. He entered the surgery and looked around.

"Of course." Dr. Lush folded his arms in front of him.

"Prendergast here has kindly offered to assist you. I think we need a full inventory of medication and other supplies, and you don't seem to be too busy," the admiral observed.

"No, not busy at all, sir," Lush whispered through gritted teeth.

"Well then, why don't you direct me to the records and you and Prendergast can start the inventory."

Lush looked at Prendergast, wondering about his offer of assistance. He knew him as a nice-enough young fellow, but in his experience the first officer wasn't the least bit interested in the infirmary.

"Not enough to do up on the bridge today?" the doctor asked his assistant.

"Something like that," Prendergast replied.

"Well," Lush sighed, "this is the last thing I need today, but at least I've got you to help."

Chapter 23

Cecelia Highton-Smith accompanied her daughter back to the girls' suite.

"Are you sure you're all right, darling?" her mother fussed as she propped her up on the sofa with some cushions. Alice-Miranda's foot was bandaged, although more as a precautionary measure than a necessity. In truth, just a Band-Aid would have been sufficient.

"I'm fine, Mummy. Dr. Lush did a wonderful job. It doesn't hurt at all."

"Now, what can I get you?" Cecelia inquired.

"I am a bit hungry. Perhaps I could order something to have here."

At that moment, the suite door flew open and Millie and Jacinta appeared.

"Oh, thank goodness you're back." Millie ran and gave Alice-Miranda a hug. "Are you okay?"

"Did it hurt a lot?" Jacinta asked. "I mean, it *was* massive."

Millie shot Jacinta a death stare.

"I'm perfectly fine. Dr. Lush was so gentle. I could hardly even feel a thing," Alice-Miranda reassured her friends.

"I'm glad." Millie nodded. "Because his bedside manner could do with some work. Come to think of it, Jacinta, you and he would make a great team."

"Why?" asked Jacinta.

"Well, you're both so reassuring." Millie raised her eyebrows. "Not!"

"I just like to tell it like it is, that's all," said Jacinta. "There's no point pretending that it was tiny when it was huge."

"It's all right, Jacinta." Alice-Miranda smiled. "I love that you're always so honest.

"Dr. Lush was a little bit cross with someone on the telephone before Mummy arrived. When I asked him why he was upset, he got a little mad with me," Alice-Miranda said.

"Darling, you mustn't meddle in other people's

business," her mother chided. "Dr. Lush is a very busy man and I'm sure he has lots of things on his mind. I think he's perfectly charming. Girls, I'm about to order Alice-Miranda a bite to eat. Would you like anything?" Cecelia asked.

Jacinta shook her head. "No, thank you, I'm full. I had spaghetti for lunch."

"I'm fine too," Millie said.

"Well, I think Alice-Miranda should probably have a rest for a little while after her lunch," Cecelia decided. "What are you girls going to do?"

"We can keep you company, Alice-Miranda," Millie replied.

"I think I might go to the gym, if that's okay," Jacinta said.

"Of course you should go," Alice-Miranda replied. "I'll be fine. If you'd rather do something else, Millie, I'll be perfectly okay on my own for an hour."

Millie said that she would stay while Alice-Miranda had her lunch and then she might go and find Lucas and Sep and see if they wanted to play a game before the storm arrived. The ship had begun rolling in the waves, and the eastern sky looked like a giant black cloth was being rolled out toward them.

"I've ordered you a sandwich, sweetheart." Cecelia sat down beside her daughter. "Mr. Winterstone will be here shortly. I have to go and see Charlotte about some of the wedding details, but I could give her a call and see if we can do that later," she fussed.

"Mummy, don't be silly. Millie's going to stay for a while and then I'll just crawl up onto my bed and have a little rest. I think the medicine has made me a bit sleepy." Alice-Miranda yawned.

"All right, darling, but I won't be far away if you need me. Mr. Winterstone can come and find me quicksticks." Cecelia kissed the top of Alice-Miranda's head. "Bye, girls. I'll be back a little later to help you choose your outfits for dinner. Remember, tonight we're in the ballroom for Bollywood night."

"I'm looking forward to that." Alice-Miranda smiled.

Cecelia Highton-Smith left the room.

"I don't think you'll be doing too much dancing," said Jacinta, looking at Alice-Miranda's foot.

"I feel fine, Jacinta, really I do. In another hour or so I'm sure I'll have forgotten all about that silly splinter," Alice-Miranda replied.

Jacinta went into the bedroom to get changed into her gym clothes, emerging a few minutes later.

"I'll see you in a while." She picked up her towel and water bottle and headed for the door.

"Bye," Alice-Miranda and Millie chorused.

A few minutes later Mr. Winterstone appeared, carrying a tray of sandwiches and a pitcher of lemon cordial.

"Hello there," Alice-Miranda said as he placed the tray on the low table in front of the couch.

"I heard you had an accident, miss," Winterstone inquired, looking at her bandaged foot.

"It was nothing, just a splinter," Alice-Miranda replied.

"That's not what I heard," said Winterstone, raising his eyebrows. "According to Miss Jacinta, who I just had the pleasure of meeting again in the corridor, you almost required an amputation."

"Oh, for goodness' sake," scoffed Millie. "That girl loves a drama. It wasn't like that at all. Alice-Miranda tripped on the deck and she got a splinter—a pretty big splinter—but it's okay now."

"Yes, I'm perfectly all right." Alice-Miranda smiled.

Winterstone pulled his tape measure from his inside coat pocket and swiftly began to set the table with exacting precision.

Millie pulled a face, wondering what on earth he was doing.

"Thank you, Mr. Winterstone. That's lovely." Alice-Miranda beamed.

"Very good, miss. Is there anything else I can get for you?"

"No, thank you. Have *you* had a good day, Mr. Winterstone?" the tiny child inquired.

"Yes, miss, as good as any other," he replied.

"What jobs do you have to do on a ship?" Alice-Miranda quizzed. "Apart from look after us, of course."

"Just the usual, I suppose," Winterstone replied. He didn't quite know where she was heading with this line of conversation.

"Well, I hope you had some time for fun?" asked Alice-Miranda.

Fun. What a strange concept, he thought. "If that will be all, miss." Winterstone retreated with a distracted air. Winterstone's life had been a series of robotic endeavors. He was a Queen's guard, and then when he got too old for the rigours of military life, he became a butler in the royal household. His life was regimented, everything in its place, everything as it should be. But this inquisitive girl stirred something inside him that he couldn't yet understand.

"He's weird," Millie said with a grimace when Winterstone was gone.

"I think he's lonely," Alice-Miranda decided. "I

can't imagine that on a great big ship like this with loads of other people you could feel alone, but I think he does. When I mentioned the word 'fun,' he looked like I'd just spoken in a foreign language. Isn't that sad? Imagine not having at least some fun every single day."

"How do you do that?" Millie asked.

"Do what?" Alice-Miranda looked at her friend.

"How do you know these things?" Millie smiled.

Alice-Miranda shrugged. "I don't know."

"Well, I'm glad that you do." Millie squeezed her friend's hand.

Chapter 24

Alice-Miranda hadn't realized how hungry she was and devoured her turkey, Brie and cranberry sauce sandwich with great gusto. She and Millie chatted about all sorts of things, but when Millie touched on the topic of Jacinta's parents, Alice-Miranda frowned.

"I wonder where her father is," Millie said.

"Yesterday I went to see Admiral Harding to find out which suite the Headlington-Bears were staying in. First Officer Prendergast said that it was Victoria and Albert, but when I found it, the nameplate only said Victoria. When I knocked, there was no answer, so I assumed they were already upstairs. But then I turned around and there was an Albert Suite on the opposite side of the hallway. When I knocked, a boy answered the door, so First Officer Prendergast might have misread the register. Anyway, we did see Mrs. Headlington-Bear at dinner. Her husband must be very busy with his work. Maybe we should go and have another look this afternoon," Alice-Miranda decided before yawning loudly.

"Yes, but you should have a rest first," Millie advised. "You look tired, and it. sounds like we'll be having another late night. I can't wait to see Mrs. Shillingsworth and Mrs. Oliver doing their Bollywood dance moves."

"Mummy told me they've been practicing for weeks, playing music while they've been doing the housework. Apparently Mrs. Oliver has the shoulder-shrug perfected, and Shilly can step-clap better than anyone. Are you going to look for Lucas and Sep?" Alice-Miranda asked.

"Yep," Millie replied.

"I think I will have a lie-down."

Alice-Miranda half walked and half hopped to the girls' bedroom. Her wound had begun a gentle throb, not painful, but just enough to let her know there had been an injury. Millie helped her onto her bed and Alice-Miranda gathered Brummel Bear beside her.

"Hello, old man," she greeted the tatty teddy. "Have you been enjoying the view?" Alice-Miranda had propped Brummel up to look out the windows before she left the suite that morning.

Staring out the wall of glass toward the coastline, Alice-Miranda could see that the ocean had been transformed from its picture-postcard stretch of blue into huge folds of waves. The ship pitched and lurched over the peaks and troughs.

"Have fun with the boys," Alice-Miranda called to her friend.

"I won't be too long." Millie waved as she headed out the door.

Alice-Miranda closed her eyes. In just a minute or so she was fast asleep. She dreamt of all manner of things: the wedding, their meeting with Mrs. Headlington-Bear and that nervous boy called Neville. She awoke with a start only half an hour later, feeling as though she was falling through a hole in the sky. It took a few seconds to realize that she *was* falling. The bed underneath her dropped without warning, and Alice-Miranda's tiny body took a second to catch up with the mattress. Outside, a coal-colored sky was shredded by lightning, and thunder like cannon fire rained from the heavens.

Alice-Miranda sat up and held on to the headboard.

Her foot seemed much better. The pain had gone completely. She decided to see if she could find Millie and Jacinta. Surely Jacinta couldn't still be in the gym—one slip and the treadmill would throw her like a cranky pony in these conditions.

Alice-Miranda stuffed her feet into a loose-fitting pair of slip-on shoes, grabbed a cardigan from the chest at the end of the room and made her way through the sitting room to the entrance hall. A couple of times the ship pitched more than she anticipated and she almost lost her balance. But being so small and with such a low center of gravity, she quickly became accustomed to the rise and fall—and was quite enjoying the challenge.

Chapter 25

Admiral Harding's inspection of the doctor's records took considerably more time than Nicholas Lush had hoped. Fortunately his methodical
attention to detail had paid off and the admiral had
nothing but praise for his work. At the same time,
First Officer Whitley Prendergast and Lush began
their inventory and ended up spending over two
hours checking off a long list of medical supplies,
noting how many of this and that were available,
down to the last Band-Aid. Admiral Harding had
long gone, telling the pair that there was a severe
storm warning and the passengers might expect to

be confined to their cabins for the evening if it turned out as badly as the forecast predicted.

Prendergast, with his constant jolly banter, had soon gotten on Nicholas's nerves. A never-ending list of questions spewed from his mouth. "So, what do you use this medication for?" "How long does it take to knock someone out with anesthetic?" "How many operations have you performed?" The fellow had driveled on and on until finally Nicholas could take it no longer and asked him to keep quiet.

Prendergast's demeanor seemed to change instantly. He shut up, all right, but he was broody and sulky and very deliberate when putting the stock back in its place.

Nicholas hadn't seen this side of the young man before. Frankly, until now he'd rather reminded him of that ridiculous child he'd just removed the splinter from—always smiling and cheerful with nothing too much of a bother. Perhaps he was seeing the real Whitley.

When finally the pair had finished the task, Whitley Prendergast shoved the inventory list under the doctor's nose and demanded that he sign it so he could get it back upstairs to the admiral.

Lush did as he was asked but laughed when Prendergast snatched it away.

"What's got into you?" he asked.

And then as if someone flipped a switch, Prendergast was back to his usual chirpy self again.

"Nothing, Doctor, nothing at all. Thank you for your assistance. I know it wasn't what you'd have liked to be doing this afternoon. Have a good evening, Dr. Lush," Prendergast gushed, and then he was gone.

Nicholas was left wondering if he shouldn't consult one of his psychology manuals about what he'd just witnessed. It seemed very peculiar indeed.

There had been several things on Nicholas's mind during the inventory. He'd been thinking about dinner and hoping that the gorgeous Ambrosia Headlington-Bear was sitting at his table as he had requested of the purser that morning. He was trying not to think about the earlier phone call but was feeling quite sick about it. "If anything were to happen to her . . . ," Nicholas murmured.

And there was the curious mystery of the young lad occupying Neville Headlington-Bear's suite, which deserved some attention right away.

Dr. Lush locked the infirmary and made his way downstairs to the Gallery Deck. He reached the Albert Suite and knocked gently at the door.

"I've come to check on Master Neville," he called.

He was expecting the steward to open up, as he had been instructed to sit with the lad, but there was no reply. Nicholas fumbled in his pocket for the master key but realized with some irritation that he'd left it sitting on his desk.

Neville Nordstrom had heard the voice outside and crept into the entrance hall to listen. He was about to open the door when Dr. Lush shouted, "I don't know who you are, lad, but I know that you're certainly not Mr. Neville Headlington-Bear, and you are most certainly not meant to be occupying this suite. I'll be back soon with the admiral. I hope you have a good explanation for impersonating a very well-respected businessman."

With that, Nicholas turned on his heel and headed back to his office to retrieve the missing key.

Neville froze. Henderson had gone to make some arrangements for some woman he'd been babbling on about. He had mentioned Neville's mother more than once too, which was very odd. His mother was not on board, but what if Henderson and Lush both thought he was somebody else? He also had a niggling feeling that something wasn't quite right about the ship. There were an awful lot of royal crests on everything, including the soap. A hot, sick feeling began to rise up his throat. What if he was on the wrong ship? Neville felt faint. The fact that the ship was rolling about in the waves was not helping.

He gathered his wits about him and decided then and there that he needed to go, before the doctor returned with the admiral. If he was in the wrong room and they thought he was impersonating someone else, he might even go to prison. Beads of perspiration formed a wet mustache on Neville's upper lip.

He raced into the bedroom and grabbed his backpack from the wardrobe. It was a jolly good thing he hadn't allowed Henderson to unpack it. As he snatched it from the floor, Neville noticed a piece of white string poking out from a shelf above. He reached up and felt around to see if it was attached to anything. Neville's hand landed on what he thought must be a laundry bag. That was odd. He hadn't even thought about sending out any washing. He gave the string a sharp pull and the bag and its contents hit the floor with a dull thud. Whatever was inside didn't sound like dirty underpants.

Neville wasn't a nosy boy—not usually. But he was curious to see what the bag contained. He undid the string and pried open the bag.

"Oh my goodness!" the nervous boy gasped. "That's not mine."

Fumbling about, all thumbs, Neville retied the

string and placed the bag back on the shelf. Except that he couldn't remember if it had been on the very top or the second from the top. His cut was throbbing and he felt like he might throw up. The doctor would be back any minute. Neville grabbed the laundry bag and threw it to the top shelf. "No, that's not where it was." He reached into his pocket for his inhaler, took two short puffs and then climbed onto the bottom shelf to try to find the laundry bag. But it was too far in and he couldn't reach it.

Neville's head was spinning. He leapt to the carpet, slammed the wardrobe door and then snatched up his backpack in one hand and his trumpet case in the other and headed for the door. He pressed his ear against the timber and listened, then checked the peephole; as far as he could tell there wasn't anyone close by. Trembling, he opened the door slowly and poked his head around. Then he ran as quickly as his legs could carry him to the end of the corridor, where another staircase led up and down. Neville decided down was a better option and fled as quickly as he could down two flights, all the while wondering where he would end up. His mind raced. He already knew he'd be in huge trouble with his parents, but that might be the least of his worries.

Chapter 26

Meanwhile, Alice-Miranda made it out of her suite to look for Millie and Jacinta. As she passed the staircase leading to the Gallery Deck, she decided she should take the opportunity to stop by and see Mr. and Mrs. Headlington-Bear. As she descended the flight of stairs, she caught sight of a snowy-haired boy running, another deck below.

"Neville!" Alice-Miranda called. The boy stopped and looked up. His eyes were huge, like two lollipops on sticks.

Neville waved Alice-Miranda away.

"Are you all right?" Alice-Miranda asked. "You look like you've seen a ghost."

Neville ran as quickly as his feet could carry him while the ship lurched and rolled beneath them.

Alice-Miranda didn't like what she had seen. Something wasn't right. The poor lad seemed terrified. She took off after him, limping down the stairs. When Alice-Miranda reached the very bottom she realized that the opulent wallpapers and plush carpets had been replaced by an industrial decor. At the end of a fluorescent-lit corridor, there was a huge steel door with a round porthole at the top—far too high for her to see through. Sounds of whooshing and clanking behind it had replaced the Muzak that flowed through the upper decks via unseen speakers.

"Neville," Alice-Miranda called over the machinery. "Where are you?"

Neville stood quivering like a five-foot blancmange in a storeroom not far from where the tiny girl was shouting.

"Neville, I'm sure that we're not supposed to be down here. Even though Aunty Gee gave us the run of the ship, she did mention that it would be best if we steered clear of the engine room, and I suspect that's where we are now. She said it's a little bit dangerous. Are you all right? Maybe I can help you?"

Neville's head was hurting, and he wanted that girl

to stop shouting at him. Without another thought he opened the door.

"In here," he squeaked.

Alice-Miranda turned and raced inside to join him. Neville hastily pulled the door shut and turned the lock on the inside.

Perspiration was trickling down his brow, and the bandage covering his wound was soaked with sweat.

Two dim wall lights shone a sickly yellow glow around the room, enabling Alice-Miranda to see that they were in some type of storeroom. It contained all manner of things, including a row of foldable beds, piles of linen in plastic packages and several writing desks and chairs similar to those in the suites. They all appeared to be brand-new.

High shelves with open mesh doors lined one side of the compartment, loaded with cutlery and crockery, candelabra and other silverware. A strong smell of mothballs made an assault on Alice-Miranda's nostrils.

She was about to speak when the ship pitched steeply and she was thrown into one of the chairs. The plastic wrap clawed at her bottom, sucking her onto the seat.

"Oh!" she exclaimed. "That's better, actually. Why

don't you sit down too, Neville, and tell me what it is you're doing down here? At least if we're sitting we have less chance of falling over."

Neville steadied himself on the arm of another chair and slid into its seat.

"It's a really big storm out there," Alice-Miranda noted. "I hope there aren't too many people feeling seasick. I've only ever felt seasick when it's been very calm with a big swell. I don't mind the waves, actually—there's something quite fun about them. But you don't look like you're having any fun at all. What's the matter?"

Neville looked at Alice-Miranda with his big blue eyes, like pools of indigo ink.

"You have to promise not to tell on me," Neville finally whispered.

"What do you mean, tell on you?" Alice-Miranda asked.

"You have to keep anything I tell you a secret," he tried again. "I think I'm in trouble."

"Trouble?" Alice-Miranda quizzed. "Why would you be in trouble? Where are your parents?"

"At home," Neville wheezed.

"What do you mean, they're at home?" Alice-Miranda tapped her finger against her cheek. "I don't understand. I thought your parents must have been friends with Uncle Lawrence, because I don't think they're friends with Aunt Charlotte or I would have met you before now."

Neville's eyes were wide. "Who's Lawrence?" he asked.

"Aunt Charlotte's fiancé, of course. Who are your parents?"

"Leonard and Sylvia Nordstrom," he mumbled.

"Oh, I don't think I know them at all," Alice-Miranda replied. "And you say that they're at home? Forgive me for asking, but why did they send you on your own?"

Neville shifted in his seat. "They didn't. I just came. Because I had to," he replied.

"Well, that's lovely, Neville, that you felt so passionate about the wedding." Alice-Miranda smiled.

Neville shook his head. "I'm not here for a wedding. I'm going to New York to meet someone. On the *Oceania,*" he squeaked.

"New York?" Alice-Miranda frowned. "I don't think so."

"Why not?" Neville looked at her, his eyes filling with tears.

"Because you're on the *Octavia* and we're going to Venice," she replied.

Chapter 27

Nicholas Lush returned to his office to find the master key. The message light on his telephone was blinking. He rather hoped it was his idiot brother telling him that she'd been located and all was well. They'd come too far to lose her now. Alas, it was Admiral Harding, and irate wouldn't have gone partway to describing the manner in which he delivered his message. Apparently the admiral had received more than twenty calls for assistance with seasickness as a result of the storm, and as Lush was nowhere to be found, he had dispatched Whitley Prendergast to begin delivering medication around the ship. Nicholas was under strict instructions to call the admiral the moment he arrived back in his office.

With some trepidation he picked up the handset and dialed the bridge.

"Lush, where on earth have you been? There are people on this ship suffering and you go and disappear. I suspect you were out schmoozing women in the bar—don't think I didn't notice your over-attentiveness with *so* many of our female guests last night. You will need to find Prendergast and see who he has already attended to," Admiral Harding barked. "Thank goodness he offered to do the rounds."

"But, sir," Lush began.

"What is it?" snapped the admiral.

"I think I might have uncovered a stowaway," Lush replied.

If Lush thought this news would distract the admiral from his irritation, he was mistaken.

"A stowaway? A *stowaway*? What a lot of nonsense," said Admiral Harding dismissively.

"But, Admiral, this morning I attended to a young boy in one of the suites, and I'm sure his name wasn't on the register when I came to write up his report."

"Was there anyone with him?" the admiral demanded.

"Yes, a steward," Lush answered.

"Well, don't you think that my stewards would know if they were attending to the right person or not?" The admiral was sick of Lush and his histrionics. "I am sure there are no stowaways on this ship, and if there were, I'd be the first to know. Now, you need to find Prendergast and get this seasickness under control. I will not have guests of Her Majesty losing their lunch because my doctor is on some wild-goose chase looking for stowaways." With that, Admiral Harding slammed the phone down.

Teddy Harding fingered the note that had just been delivered to the bridge. He had far more important things on his mind than looking for alleged stowaways. The fates of more than five hundred people rested in his hands.

Chapter 28

"**D**on't you worry about a thing." Alice-Miranda smiled. "I have to find my friends and get to dinner, but I'll bring you something to eat in a little while. I promise, Neville, we can work this out. I'm sure that you won't be in trouble."

Alice-Miranda patted him gently on the shoulder. Her reassuring smile made him feel ever so slightly less anxious, although his parents would likely still ground him for life when he got home—if he ever got home, that is.

Alice-Miranda had listened to Neville Nordstrom and his wonderful story. She'd never met anyone so passionate about conservation. He shouldn't be in trouble, she thought. He should be given an award! And she couldn't believe it either when he said that his online friend was heading for Spain, just as he was steaming toward the USA—well, except that now he wasn't. Alice-Miranda's brain had gone into overdrive—there was already a plan bubbling away.

She promised not to tell anyone about him. After all, he had written his parents a letter explaining where he had gone—it's just that he wasn't really where he said he would be.

"You're not going to telephone my parents, are you?" Neville asked, his eyes filling with tears.

"No. It might be best they think you're still heading for New York. We can't let them know where you really are, or it might spoil everything for Aunt Charlotte and Uncle Lawrence. Where exactly do you live, Neville?" Alice-Miranda asked.

"Castelldefels," he replied. "Just by the beach, down the road from the country club."

"Oh my goodness, that's perfect!" Alice-Miranda gasped.

"Why?" Neville frowned.

"Because I know someone who lives there too. I'm sure that if I ask her she'll help get a message to your parents. At least then they'll know you're all right. All of the calls from the ship are monitored anyway—

I mean, Aunty Gee can't be too careful with security. But there's a mail pickup each morning, and I can get a letter to my friend with another letter for your parents inside. I'm sure she'll help us."

Neville was puzzled. "But why don't you just write to my parents instead?"

"I don't know if they'd believe me, and at least this way, my friend can back me up."

"So, you promise you won't tell anyone I'm here?" Neville begged. "I've made such a botch of it. I didn't mean to get on the wrong ship. It's just that I met a lady on the dock. She asked me where my parents were and I sort of panicked, I think. She was very kind but she seemed in a hurry, and I didn't want to upset her," he explained.

"Don't worry, Neville, I promise," Alice-Miranda told him. "That lady you met on the dock. What did she look like?"

"Well, she was very regal-looking. In fact, she sort of looked like . . . Oh gosh. It was the Queen, wasn't it?"

Alice-Miranda nodded. Poor Neville couldn't have felt more foolish.

"My mum would be so excited to know that I was talking to Queen Georgiana." He managed a tight smile.

"See, Neville, things will work out," Alice-Miranda assured him. She just had to work out exactly how.

Chapter 29

Alice-Miranda ran back upstairs to her suite to find Millie patting Cecelia's arm, apparently trying to calm her down, and Jacinta ready to head off on a search party.

Millie ran to Alice-Miranda's side. "Where have you been?"

"I had a sleep and then I went for a walk to find you," Alice-Miranda replied.

"Oh, darling, I was so worried." Cecelia strode across the room and gave her tiny daughter a hug.

"I'm so sorry, Mummy. I know it's pretty nasty out there," Alice-Miranda apologized. "I didn't mean to worry you."

A tear slid down her mother's face. "It's just the seas are so big and the ship has been pitching and rolling. I had started to think you'd gone overboard," she said, and sniffed.

"Please don't cry, Mummy. I'm fine." Alice-Miranda raced to the bathroom and returned with a tissue for Cecelia.

"I was nearly swept away coming back from the gym," announced Jacinta.

"Really?" said Alice-Miranda. "On an enclosed deck?"

"Well, I slipped in a puddle of water," Jacinta confessed, "and I almost fell over."

"Goodness me. You and Mummy could both win Academy Awards for your dramatic performances." Alice-Miranda rolled her eyes. "Anyway, I'm back now, and it looks as though there's a break in the weather."

A vivid rainbow stretched from one end of the bay to the other, perfectly framing the coastline in the distance.

"Oh, look at that!" Millie rushed to the window. "It's beautiful."

The storm seemed to have passed, and the boiling seas were settling to a hiss.

"Well, I'm just glad you're safe, darling." Cecelia

smiled at her daughter and hugged her tightly. "Now, we must start getting ready for the party."

Cecelia Highton-Smith helped the girls select their outfits for the evening's festivities. She had made sure that there was a range of saris packed into Alice-Miranda's luggage. Millie selected a beautiful emerald-green with sequins, Jacinta went for hot pink with a silver edging and Alice-Miranda found herself in heavenly pale blue with delicate gold embroidery. Shilly appeared at the door and offered to do the girls' hair so Cecelia could go and get ready herself.

"I love your sari, Mrs. Shillingsworth," said Jacinta as she admired Shilly's red dress, which had more decorations than most Christmas trees.

"Thank you, my dear," Shilly replied. "I think it's quite fetching myself. I certainly understand the attraction—this type of garment tends to hide all of the lumps and bumps of age."

Millie looked at her. "But you're not fat, Shilly."

"Let's just say, dear, that modern corsetry does a wonderful job." Shilly winked. "What would you like me to do with your hair, Alice-Miranda?"

"It's all right, Shilly. I can manage. Spend your time on Millie and Jacinta. I've got something I have to do," Alice-Miranda called from the bedroom.

She needed to write that letter and make sure it was in the mail first thing in the morning. Alice-Miranda retreated to the writing desk, where she pulled out a piece of notepaper embellished with the royal crest.

Dear Sloane,
I hope this letter finds you well . . .

Alice-Miranda finished her letter and began a new note to Neville's parents explaining the situation.

Winterstone appeared at the bedroom door. "You're very focused, miss."

"I just want to get a letter into the post first thing in the morning, if I may?" Alice-Miranda asked.

"Is everything all right?" Winterstone frowned.

"Yes, just lovely, Mr. Winterstone," Alice-Miranda replied.

Mrs. Shillingsworth emerged from the ensuite bathroom with Jacinta and Millie in tow.

Alice-Miranda slipped the second envelope inside the first and sealed it up.

She looked up and admired Millie's and Jacinta's dos. "Your hair looks lovely."

"Thanks," Millie replied. "Who are you writing to?"

"Sloane," Alice-Miranda replied.

"Urgh, I don't know why you'd be wasting your time, Alice-Miranda," Jacinta said. "You know she's a cheat and a liar."

"She can't be all bad, Jacinta. I mean, look at Sep— he's just about one of the nicest boys I've ever met and he's her brother."

"I see what you mean. But he must be the odd one out in his family. Like me in mine," said Jacinta.

"Well, come along, girls," Shilly interrupted. "It's time we princesses made our way to the ball."

Alice-Miranda handed the letter to Winterstone.

"I'll make sure it gets in the mail run," he said with a nod.

"Thank you." Alice-Miranda beamed.

Chapter 30

Three rooms farther along the hallway, Lady Sarah Adams, having completely overcome her nasty bout of seasickness, was putting the finishing touches to her gorgeous pale pink ensemble. Her sari shimmered with thousands of tiny crystals, and her blond hair had been curled into loose ringlets.

"Mummy, you look beautiful," her daughter Annie complimented her.

"Which necklace are you going to wear?" her younger daughter, Poppy, asked.

"Daddy's just getting my diamonds from the safe, girls." Lady Sarah turned around to find her husband, Lord Robert, standing in the doorway to the main bedroom. His eyebrows were knitted tightly together.

"Is everything all right?"

"Yes, darling, of course. Would you mind popping in here for a minute?"

"Girls, why don't you go and brush your hair?" their mother instructed.

"What's the matter?" Sarah entered the bedroom. Her husband quickly shut the door behind them.

"What jewelry did you bring with you, darling?"

"Um, gosh, loads, you know me, Robert. My diamond bracelet and necklace, the Cartier necklace . . . Let me think. There were three dress rings and of course the sapphires—a whole set—and my emerald earrings, a brooch and my emerald tiara for the wedding." Sarah stared at the wardrobe that contained the safe, ticking the list off in her mind. "And my usual pearls, gold chains, bracelets and my watch," she said, glancing at her wrist.

"Well, I hate to tell you this, sweetheart, but it's all gone." Robert pushed the racks of gowns to one side to reveal an empty safe.

"What do you mean, it's all gone?" Sarah gasped. "How? We're in the middle of the ocean, for goodness' sake! We need to call security right away."

"No!" Robert shook his head. He was gripping a folded piece of paper tightly in his hand.

"Of course we have to. I'm not letting some petty officer make off with my lovely jewels!" Sarah cried.

"I'm afraid, darling, we mustn't tell anyone." Robert sat down on the bed and passed his wife the paper.

As Lady Sarah read the note's contents, her face drained of color. Even her bright pink lipstick took on a decidedly pasty tinge.

She stifled a cry. "This can't be true. Do you think they're serious?"

"We can't risk it. We mustn't tell a soul. At least, not while we're on board—who knows what listening devices these brutes have?" Robert whispered into his wife's ear.

The pair embraced tightly.

"I wonder if it's the same gang that's been stealing all those Russian jewels. I read something about that in the newspaper just last week," Robert commented.

"But none of my jewels are Russian. Well, not as far as I know. It can't be that," Sarah replied.

She looked at the paper again and handed it back to her husband.

"We mustn't let the girls out of our sight," Sarah said in a choked voice, and then began to cry.

{195}

"Come on, darling. Everything has to remain as normal as possible. We mustn't arouse any suspicion." Robert handed Sarah a tissue and she went to the bathroom to fix her smudged makeup.

"Are you all right?" Robert asked as she emerged.

"No, not really. I feel sick to my stomach." Sarah managed a tight smile. "But I'll be fine. I don't have a choice."

"That's my girl." Robert took his wife by the hand and they emerged from their bedroom to call Annie and Poppy. Together the family made their way to the ballroom.

"Mummy, you're not wearing your diamonds," Poppy commented as they headed along the hallway.

"No, darling, it was far too much with all these crystals. You know I like to take the less-is-more approach."

Her young daughter seemed satisfied with her mother's response for now. But how long it would take before someone noticed that the usually bejeweled Lady Sarah was missing her baubles was anyone's guess.

Chapter 31

"Master Neville, I found your trumpet case,"
Henderson called as he entered the suite.
He had been shocked to see it poking out from behind a flowerpot in the storeroom beside the ballroom. He knew how attached the boy was to it. But
there was no mistaking the brown leather case with
its tatty corners and huge smiley-face sticker in the
middle of the lid.

Henderson placed the case beside the end of the
couch and walked into the bedroom. There was no
sign of Neville. The bathroom door was open, but he
wasn't in there either.

Perhaps his mother had finally taken an interest and insisted he escort her to dinner.

Henderson attended to his evening duties, turning back the bedclothes and fluffing the pillows. He switched on the bedside lamps before turning his attention to the bathroom, where he hung up the towels and tidied the vanity. His last chore of the evening was to rearrange the cushions on the couch. He looked at Neville's trumpet case and decided that the young boy would probably feel better if his beloved instrument was tucked away safely under the pillows, which is exactly what he did. That way, Master Neville would find it as soon as he hopped into bed.

"And I'll just collect the laundry," Henderson said to himself as he opened the wardrobe doors. "Don't want to get myself into any more trouble with the boss."

Upstairs in the ballroom, the dance floor was packed with guests shimmying and shaking to the sounds of a Bollywood beat. The saris were spectacular, with literally thousands of sparkling sequins and crystals. While Lady Sarah felt quite naked without her jewels, there was enough bling to ensure that no one would notice—tonight, at least.

Vladimir and his staff had again outdone themselves with an Indian feast fit for a king, or in this case, a queen.

On the long smorgasbord tables, kormas and koftas sat alongside naan breads and chutneys, curries of all intensities and fragrant rice. Alice-Miranda spotted Mrs. Oliver making some notes about one particularly tasty dish.

"Oh, I simply have to find out how Chef Vladimir gets that consistency," she gushed at Alice-Miranda.

Over at the main table, Cecelia Highton-Smith was asking Admiral Harding if he'd seen Dr. Lush.

"No, we had quite a few passengers take ill this afternoon in the storm, my dear. The doctor won't be off duty for hours, I should think," the admiral commented.

"That's a pity," Cecelia replied. "I had asked him to join us for dinner. He did a wonderful job of pulling that horrid splinter from Alice-Miranda's foot."

"Yes, I heard the poor lass had a nasty lump of wood embedded between her toes," Admiral Harding said with a deep frown. "I am terribly sorry, Cecelia—there are men upstairs as we speak, sanding and repolishing the decking around the pool. We simply can't have that on the *Octavia*."

"Please don't fuss, Admiral. Alice-Miranda's absolutely fine," Cecelia replied. "If I know my daughter, I'm sure she'll be up dancing any minute."

But that was not quite the case. Aware that it had been a while since she had seen Neville, Alice-Miranda decided to pop out to the kitchen and ask if Chef Vladimir could supply her with some leftovers. She had already placed two dinner rolls in a napkin and was holding on to them tightly. Millie spied her leaving. "Where are you going?"

"I just need to take something for the pain in my foot," said Alice-Miranda. She hated telling untruths, but her foot *was* starting to throb a little, and she didn't think she'd be able to dance. Maybe she should ask her mother for a tablet.

"I'll come with you," Millie offered.

"No, it's all right. I won't be long." Alice-Miranda disappeared out the side door and made her way to the kitchen.

Unlike the first time she had been there, tonight the atmosphere was electric. Vladimir barked orders at his men, who were rushing from hot plate to oven and back again.

Alice-Miranda marched into the galley. "Hello, Chef Vladimir."

"Who zaid that?" he exploded.

"Excuse me, Chef Vladimir, it's me, Alice-Miranda—down here," she called.

Vladimir gazed at the tiny child. "You should not be here. Get out!" he roared.

"I am sorry, Chef Vladimir, I know you're terribly busy, but I wanted to know if I might have a take-away pack of some of the dinner, please?" she continued.

"Takeaway? What on earth you want that for?" he demanded.

"Well, you see, I have a friend who couldn't come tonight, and I know that he would love to try some of your dishes. Truly, sir, I don't think I've ever had Indian food as good as this, and believe me, I've spent quite a lot of time with Mummy and Daddy's friend Prince Shivaji in his palace in Jaipur. He has wonderful chefs, but I think you could teach them a thing or two." Alice-Miranda beamed.

"You think so, do you?" Vladimir's chest puffed out like a peacock's.

"Oh yes, Chef Vladimir. Your vegetable kofta was amazing."

"You!" Vladimir pointed at a pasty young chef. "Get this child anything she wants. Deliver for room service."

"Oh no, that won't be necessary, Chef Vladimir.

I'd like to deliver it to my friend myself. Takeaway containers will be just fine," Alice-Miranda confirmed.

Vladimir frowned. "I don't believe we have such thing in my kitchen."

"You must have some plastic storage containers, Chef Vladimir. I promise I'll bring them back afterward," Alice-Miranda assured the chef.

"Where is this friend of yours, and why he not come to the party?" Vladimir asked, his dark eyes narrowing.

"He hasn't been feeling well since the storm, so he's stayed in for the night. I just wanted to take him some dinner, and the room service trays are far too big for me to manage on my own," Alice-Miranda said. This was proving more difficult than she had first imagined.

"Well, I get one of these idiots to help you, then. I can't let my food go into plastic container. Iz not right. Will contaminate taste," Vladimir insisted.

"All right then, Chef Vladimir." Alice-Miranda looked up at him with her brown eyes as big as saucers. "I'll come back in a few minutes to let you know which room he's in."

Alice-Miranda knew very well that Neville's room was the Albert Suite, but she thought she'd better convince him to return there from his hidey-hole before the room service was sent.

"Telephone the number, miss, and stay out of this kitchen. Iz no place for child—there are men with knives."

"Goodbye, Chef Vladimir," she called. "Thank you very much."

Vladimir stared at her as she scampered from the kitchen. There was a strange feeling buzzing on his lips—something he hadn't felt for a very long time.

One of the chefs prodded another who was standing beside him. "Did you see that?" he whispered.

"What?" the other replied.

"Old Vlad the Impaler—I think he almost cracked a smile." The cook grinned.

"What you grinning about? Imbecile! You know the rules. There is nothing to smile about in my kitchen!" Vladimir thumped his fist on the nearest bench and stormed off to shout at someone else.

Alice-Miranda exited the kitchen and headed along the corridor toward the stairs.

"Alice-Miranda!" a voice called out behind her. "Where are you going?"

She turned to see Millie approaching.

"I thought you said you were just taking some medicine."

"I do need some medicine, I promise, but I have something else I need to do too. I was going to tell you once I had worked things out a little bit more. But come with me and I'll explain on the way." Alice-Miranda took Millie's hand and the two girls made their way downstairs.

Alice-Miranda told Millie how she had come to meet Neville and what a nervous boy he was and that he now thought he was in huge trouble for being on the wrong ship.

"That *is* a pretty outrageous story," Millie agreed. "Are you sure he's telling you the truth? Maybe he's a miniature paparazzo sent to creep into the party and get the best pictures for *Gloss and Goss*." Millie smiled at her own cleverness.

"I'm sure he's telling the truth," Alice-Miranda replied. "The poor boy quivers like Jell-O most of the time, and it took every ounce of strength for him to explain how he came to be here. Dr. Lush had to treat him earlier today, and he has a couple of stitches in his brow—"

"What happened to him?" Millie interrupted.

"He had an unfortunate collision with a cereal bowl. Anyway, Dr. Lush must have worked out that Neville shouldn't have been there, and he yelled at him through the door and said that he was going to tell Admiral Harding. That's when I spotted him fleeing down here."

"Why don't we just go and tell your parents and then·he can join in the party? He sounds like he could do with some fun."

"Yes, I thought so too. I suggested that to Neville, but he's so scared he doesn't want me to tell anyone. I have a feeling bringing you along is going to cause him a great deal of distress. Anyway, I have a plan to get a message to his parents so that *hopefully* they won't call the police or cause too much of a fuss. We really don't want to attract any attention to the ship, so I've written a letter."

"A letter?" Millie quizzed.

"Yes. Neville's parents live right down the road from Sep's mum and dad, so I wrote to Sloane asking her if she could deliver a letter to them," Alice-Miranda replied.

Millie shook her head. "Oh, you know she won't help. She hates us."

"Well, I can only try," said Alice-Miranda. "And you know I don't think Sloane's as bad as all that."

"Well, I hope you're right." Millie skidded down the last step onto the metal floor. "Isn't that the engine room?"

"Yes, through there." Alice-Miranda pointed at the

large steel door. The roar of the engines had settled to a hum as the ship anchored off the coast for the night.

"Is *that* where he is?" Millie asked.

"No, he's at the end of this hallway in a storeroom." The smaller girl led Millie down the dimly lit corridor.

The girls reached the storeroom and Alice-Miranda knocked gently at the door.

"Neville," she whispered. "It's me." Alice-Miranda turned to Millie. "Just wait here for a moment while I explain about you to Neville."

The lock turned and Neville opened the door. Alice-Miranda thrust two dinner rolls into his hands and slipped into the room.

"I'm sorry. It's all I could get at the moment. And I have something to tell you," Alice-Miranda began. "I know that I promised not to tell anyone about you, but it's just that my best friend, Millie, saw me coming out of the kitchen and wondered where I was going."

Neville gulped. His throat felt as if there was half a loaf of bread wedged in it, and he hadn't yet taken a bite of his rolls. Streams of perspiration began to run down his forehead, and he reached inside his pocket and took two puffs of his inhaler.

"It's all right, Neville, I promise it is. Millie won't tell anyone about you. She's just outside and I'd really like you to meet her." Alice-Miranda turned around and unsnapped the lock. She beckoned for Millie to come in.

The red-haired girl scurried inside and Alice-Miranda locked the door behind her. In the yellow light, Neville's already pale complexion had taken on a chalky texture.

"Hello," Millie said.

Neville managed a gulp.

"Millie is my best friend in the whole world, Neville, and she's very good at keeping secrets. She won't tell anyone about you," Alice-Miranda reassured him.

"She's right, Neville. I'm good at keeping secrets. One day, when you're feeling better, we'll tell you all about Miss Hephzibah. That was a huge secret to keep."

Alice-Miranda guided Neville and Millie to sit down so she could explain her attempts at getting Neville some more food.

"You were in the Albert Suite, weren't you?" Alice-Miranda said carefully. "I think that's where our friend Jacinta's father is meant to be. How long were you there?"

"Until this afternoon, when you saw me." Neville

had finished the first roll and was almost through the second.

"So, how many people know you were there?" Alice-Miranda asked.

"That doctor who came after me and Henderson, the steward," Neville replied.

"And you're sure that's all?" Alice-Miranda asked. Neville nodded.

"I wonder where on earth Mr. Headlington-Bear is, then. He's meant to be on the ship, and clearly he's not if you managed to stay in his suite for the past couple of days. And I wonder why your butler, Henderson, didn't realize that you were the wrong person. That's very shabby security," Alice-Miranda thought aloud.

"Please," Neville begged. "You promised that you wouldn't tell anyone about me. And you've already told her." He pointed at Millie. "I don't want to get in trouble, and I didn't mean to get on the wrong ship."

Fat tears wobbled in Neville's eyes and spilled onto his cheeks.

"It's all right, Neville. I take my promises seriously," Alice-Miranda soothed. Her mind was racing. She had thought for a moment that perhaps it would be best to let her father in on Neville and his predicament. Daddy would know exactly how to help. But then, she really didn't want to cause a fuss before the wedding, and poor Neville was so upset.

"What about if we go back upstairs to your suite and I have the food delivered there?" Alice-Miranda asked. "We know Mr. Headlington-Bear's not using it, and if you're missing, Mr. Henderson will likely raise the alarm anyway."

Neville hunched farther under the desk. "I can't go back. That doctor, he knows I shouldn't be there, and he said that he was going to tell the admiral."

Alice-Miranda bit her lip. "I'm sure I can explain to Dr. Lush. He's a perfectly reasonable man, and I really don't understand what he would have to gain from telling on you."

"But—" Neville began.

Alice-Miranda put her finger to her lips. She thought she could hear voices—and they were getting closer.

"What's that?" Neville whispered.

"Someone's trying to open the door," Alice-Miranda said.

"Quick!" Millie shoved Neville into the depths of the storeroom and grabbed Alice-Miranda's hand. The three of them hid underneath a writing desk that was pushed into the back corner. Neville snatched his trumpet case from the floor beside him but remembered that his backpack was sitting next to the chair he had been sitting on.

"I've got to get my bag," he wheezed.

"It's all right, I'll get it." Alice-Miranda raced out and returned with the backpack just as the key jiggled in the lock and the door opened.

Neville's heart hammered inside his chest. Alice-Miranda thought he might pass out. Jammed in together under the desk, the children couldn't see who had entered the room. Alice-Miranda hoped they were just after some supplies and would disappear again in a minute.

The door clicked shut and Alice-Miranda heard the lock turn. She was just about to hop up when a voice growled.

"I can't believe you. Are you completely thick?"

"No!" another replied.

Alice-Miranda listened intently.

In the darkness under the desk Alice-Miranda could see only the whites of Neville's eyes.

"Why did you pack her into a trumpet case, you idiot? I'd have thought she deserved better than that."

"It was inconspicuous," the other fellow replied. "And I'm in a band."

"I just can't believe it. I knew I should have taken care of her myself. We've carried her all the way from Russia, she's the most precious thing in the world, and now you've gone and lost her," the first voice berated. "Why didn't you keep her in your room?"

"Well, I did, but then my roommate came in and saw it and he said that all the instruments had to be left in the storeroom. I took her up, then I took her back down and hid her, but those cabins aren't very roomy, you know. He must have found her and taken her back up again when I wasn't there. It's not my fault. Someone must have picked her up. She can't have gone far," the second man replied.

"If you don't find her before we get to Venice . . . I just don't want to think about it," the first man spat. "What did the case look like?"

"Very shabby and quite beaten up, really. It's that old one I had when I was a boy, with the giant smiley-face sticker in the middle. I can't imagine that anyone would want it. It's not worth anything."

"Not worth anything! Are you kidding? The contents of that case are worth more to me than anything." The first man seemed to stifle a sob.

"You're being a bit dramatic, aren't you, brother?"

"Dramatic! *Dramatic?*" the first man hissed. "I'll give you dramatic!"

"Well, I'm sure the case can't have gone far," the other man spoke.

"Hang on. Did you say a smiley-face sticker?"

"Yes, I put it there myself about fifteen years ago."

"I've seen that case. That boy, the one who's in the Albert Suite. He's got it!" the first man exclaimed. "He's a stowaway *and* a thief! Come on, let's go back up there now and get it. He'll have some explaining to do . . ."

Alice-Miranda's mind was a whirl. Russia . . . *She* . . . the most precious thing in the world . . . What did it all mean—and why did it sound so familiar?

"I've got a key," the first voice hissed. "Hurry up, you numbskull."

The door opened with a snap and the men exited the storeroom, locking it again from the outside.

"What was all that about?" Millie said as she hopped out from under the desk.

Neville's clenched hands were wet and he felt as though he might throw up.

"I don't know, exactly." Alice-Miranda pushed herself from under the desk and reached out to help Neville to his feet. The children moved back toward the less crowded end of the storeroom. "The first man—I recognized his voice."

"It was Dr. Lush!" Millie exclaimed.

"He's the man who came looking for me," Neville confirmed. "But what does my trumpet case have to do with anything?"

"And who was the other man? He called him 'brother,'" said Alice-Miranda.

Millie's eyes widened and she looked like she was about to explode. "Alice-Miranda! It was them. I bet they've got those jewels your father and Aunty Gee were talking about at dinner the other night. They said they'd carried her all the way from Russia—the most precious thing in the world."

Alice-Miranda looked doubtful. "Millie, I'm sure that's not it at all."

"Why not? It makes sense, doesn't it? Who would suspect they were carrying one of the world's most precious diamonds in a battered old trumpet case?" Millie asked.

"Do you really think the doctor is a thief?" Neville's eyes were wide.

"Of course not," Alice-Miranda replied. "I'm sure there's a perfectly good explanation."

"But there's something else I haven't told you," Neville wheezed.

"What is it?" Alice-Miranda noticed that the boy was shivering despite the temperature in the room being positively tropical.

"When I was getting my bag out of the wardrobe, I saw something. At first I thought it was a laundry bag, but then I pulled it down, and it didn't have laundry in it."

"Well, come on, Neville," Millie coaxed. "Out with it. What was in the bag?"

"Well . . ." Neville gulped. "There was a towel, and inside the towel there were . . . jewels."

"Jewels? What sort of jewels?" Alice-Miranda asked, aware that it had taken all his strength to say as much as he just had.

"I don't know, but they were sparkly and there seemed to be quite a lot of them."

"I wonder who they belong to?" Alice-Miranda's thoughts were racing.

Millie had already made up her mind. "They're stolen, of course. Dr. Lush probably hid them there." Alice-Miranda opened her mouth to object, but Millie carried on. "So are you sure that's a trumpet in there?" she gestured toward Neville's battered case.

Neville swallowed hard. "It's not a trumpet."

"What is it, then?" Millie demanded. "Do you have their case?"

"No! It's a Spanish Greenish Black-tip Euchloe Bazae," Neville replied.

"A what?" Millie asked. "Is that a type of jewel?"

"Well, some people think so." Alice-Miranda smiled. "It's a butterfly."

"A butterfly? Well, it won't last long in there," Millie said.

"No, it's in a frame and it used to belong to Neville's grandfather," Alice-Miranda explained. "That's how he came to be interested in them in the first place. And would you believe that this particular butterfly is meant to be extinct. But clever Neville's found a whole colony of them and he needs help, and that's why he's on the ship."

"I don't understand." Millie bit her lip. "Why did Neville need to come on the *Octavia* to get help with butterflies?"

"No, he's not meant to be on the *Octavia*. He thought he was going to America on another ship, but Aunty Gee persuaded him that he should get on board and here he is."

"This is very confusing," Millie sighed.

Neville flipped open the locks and pulled a timber frame from the center of the padded case. He passed it to Millie. A tiny, perfect butterfly, greenish-black, was mounted under the glass. He pulled out an envelope full of photographs and passed them to Alice-Miranda.

"Neville showed me these before. He took them just last month. See, Millie—it's the same butterfly."

"Oh, they're beautiful, Neville," Millie said admiringly. "You're a very good photographer."

Neville managed a tight smile.

"But why didn't you just telephone someone at a university or something?" Millie asked. "I'm sure there are people who are into butterflies who could have helped you."

"I did, but my Spanish is so bad they couldn't understand me and said that I was a mischief-maker," Neville whispered. "I tried to tell some people in the butterfly club too, but they said I must have been mistaken. But I'm not. I know I'm not, and I just wanted someone to believe me. This habitat is going to be bulldozed next month for houses."

"Why didn't you tell your parents, then? Couldn't they help you?" Millie asked.

"My dad thinks I'm at soccer training when I'm hunting butterflies. I didn't want to disappoint him, and I don't think he'd understand at all. He's not exactly into conservation. You see, he'll quite likely be the one supplying the bulldozers. He's gone into business with a man called Smedley Sykes, and they're doing lots of developments."

"Sykes? Did you say Sykes?" Alice-Miranda asked.

"Well, that figures." Millie frowned. "You'd better convince your butterfly friends to move quick-smart. I bet that's Sloane's father, and if he's anything like her and her mother, your butterfly habitat doesn't stand a chance."

Alice-Miranda could see the fear on Neville's face. "We don't know for sure," she said soothingly.

"So why were you going to America?" Millie asked.

"I met someone on the Internet in our club chat room, and I know he can help me," Neville began.

"But why do you need to go there?" Millie asked. "Why don't you just tell him?"

"Because he won't talk to me anymore." Neville bit his thumbnail.

Millie sighed. "I really don't understand any of this."

"Don't worry, Millie. I'll explain the rest later. I'm sure it will all work out for Neville. And just imagine—he'll be an environmental hero!" Alice-Miranda added.

The corners of Neville's mouth turned ever so slightly upward.

"I think we should go back to your suite soon," Alice-Miranda said.

"But how?"

"I'll have a chat with Dr. Lush straight away and

see if we can get things cleared up," Alice-Miranda replied.

"No!" Millie cried. "What if he has a gun? Criminals usually carry weapons, and you might not be as lucky as the last time."

"The last time?" Neville exclaimed. "Do you make a habit of this sort of thing?"

"Of course not, Neville." Alice-Miranda shook her head. "I'm sure Dr. Lush isn't dangerous. He was very gentle when he removed that splinter from my foot today. There has to be a perfectly reasonable explanation. I'm sure of it."

Chapter 32

"**T**here you are, Lush." Admiral Harding walked toward the doctor, who was hurrying along the corridor on his way to the Albert Suite. Nicholas elbowed the tall man with the unmissable hair beside him, who, after some terse words, changed course to slope back to the other end of the hallway and disappeared from sight.

"Sir," Lush addressed the admiral.

"I've just heard that Her Majesty is not feeling the best. You need to get to the Royal Suite immediately," Admiral Harding commanded. "It could be one of her allergic reactions, by the sounds of things. Heaven only knows how we ended up with crustaceans on the ship—if that's what it is. You'd better be prepared to stay with her through the night. I've already sent Prendergast. Such a reliable young fellow."

"But, sir, I just need to—"

"Dr. Lush, are you telling me that you're not going to attend to our monarch as a matter of urgency?" The old man raised his left eyebrow.

"Of course, sir. I'll go straight there." Nicholas Lush sighed. He couldn't believe he was so close and now this.

"You'd do well to have an attitude adjustment, Lush," Admiral Harding advised. "Sighing and pouting are two things I will not put up with on this ship."

"Yes, sir," the doctor mumbled as he scurried away to attend to the Queen.

Alice-Miranda, Millie and Neville left the safety of the storeroom and scampered upstairs to the Gallery Deck. Just as they arrived on the landing, Admiral Harding strode along the hallway.

"Good evening, young ladies, young man," the admiral greeted the group. Neville thought he might throw up on the officer's gleaming black shoes. "Have you had enough of the party already?"

"Oh no, Admiral, we're having a wonderful time." Alice-Miranda smiled. "Have you seen Dr. Lush?"

"Yes, just a few minutes ago I sent him up to take care of Her Majesty. She's not feeling the best."

"Was he with anyone?" Alice-Miranda asked.

"No, not when I spoke to him. But come to think of it, I saw that extremely tall fellow with the incredible hair scuttling off in the other direction. Don't know what he was doing with Lush. He's in the band. I introduced myself to him just yesterday. I'm sure he should be upstairs working right now." The admiral rubbed his chin. "I don't know. It's so hard to get good help these days."

"Oh, we met him too, when we were exploring yesterday. His name's Alex," Alice-Miranda replied.

"He must be Dr. Lush's brother," Millie whispered.

The admiral didn't hear her. "Yes, that's it. Alexander Lushkov. Russian name, I think. Mmm." He thought for a moment. "You haven't observed any unusual behavior among the passengers today, have you?"

Neville moved in behind Millie and stared at the floor, willing a hole to open up and swallow him into the depths below.

"What sort of behavior?" Millie asked.

The admiral cleared his throat. "Just anything out of the ordinary. People acting strangely, as though they don't really belong."

"No, not at all," said Alice-Miranda. "Has something happened?"

The admiral shook his head. "No, no, just a feeling, that's all."

"Oh, really, do you get them too?" Alice-Miranda stared at the old man intently. "It happens to me quite often, and you know, I have had a strange feeling about a few things on the ship since we arrived. I just can't say exactly what they are yet."

Admiral Harding nodded; then a horrified look passed over his face. "Good heavens, lad, have those trainers been through a war?" The old man continued to stare at Neville's grubby shoes. "Have you got a voice, son?"

"Y-y-y-es, sir," Neville wheezed.

"Are you unwell?" The admiral strode forward and peered around Millie's shoulder, where Neville was trying to make himself invisible. He was holding his trumpet case behind his leg, and Millie had his backpack slung over her shoulder. Fortunately both seemed to go unnoticed by the admiral.

"N-n-n-no, s-s-sir," Neville stammered.

"You're not a stowaway, are you, lad? Dr. Lush was trying to tell me we had a boy hiding on board the ship. I can't imagine anything more preposterous, now, can you?"

"Oh, Admiral Harding." Alice-Miranda walked forward and looped her arm with the old man's. "What a thing to say! That's Neville, and he's with us."

"Oh, of course he is." The admiral nodded and then whispered, "Are his parents friends with your parents?"

"Not exactly," Alice-Miranda replied.

"Oh, they must be with the Ridleys," the admiral decided. Alice-Miranda did not correct him. "Anyway, my dear, I must be off to do the rounds. Hurry back to the party. There was some rather fierce dancing going on up there—your dear Shilly and Mrs. Oliver were giving the young ones a great run for their money."

Alice-Miranda walked the admiral to the other end of the corridor.

"And if you notice anything unusual, you will come and see me on the bridge. . . ." The admiral's voice floated back down the hall as he walked away with his tiny guide.

Millie and Neville stopped and pretended to admire a cubist Picasso adorning the wall beside the Albert Suite. When the admiral had shuffled off around the corner, Alice-Miranda raced back to join her friends.

Neville was fumbling with his key. He jiggled it

into the lock and opened the door, and the children hurried inside.

Millie raced into the bedroom and wrenched open the wardrobe door.

"No, the other end," Neville panted. "I threw the bag onto the top shelf."

Millie scampered onto the lower shelves and hauled herself up as far as she could. She felt around for the laundry bag, but there was only empty space.

Alice-Miranda stood on the bed and jumped up to see if she could catch a glimpse of anything.

"There's nothing there." She jumped several more times to be sure.

"But I threw it up there just before I left." Neville looked as though he was about to cry. "You do believe me, don't you?"

"Of course we do, Neville." Alice-Miranda hopped down off the bed and placed her arm around his shoulders. Neville flinched. He wasn't used to being consoled by girls.

"Dr. Lush must have taken it," Millie decided. "He was on his way up here. That's the only explanation."

"You heard the admiral, Millie," Alice-Miranda said. "Dr. Lush is with Aunty Gee."

Neville's stomach growled like a hungry kitten.

"I think we should order you some food before you pass out." Alice-Miranda skipped into the sitting room, picked up the telephone and dialed through to the kitchen. A few moments later she declared, "It will be here shortly," and placed the handset back into the cradle.

"If Dr. Lush thinks you have his trumpet case, maybe we should hide *this,* in case he comes back and takes it." Millie picked up Neville's case and began looking for a suitable place to conceal it. "What about in that cupboard next to the minibar?" she suggested. The boy nodded.

Millie closed the cupboard door and plonked down on the couch next to Neville, who was holding his head in his hands.

"This is such a mess," he mumbled.

"It's all right, Neville," said Alice-Miranda as she opened the door of the minibar. "How about I pour you a cold drink? I don't know about you, but I'm rather thirsty."

"May I have lemonade?" Millie asked.

There was a sharp rap on the cabin door.

"Oh no, it's them!" Neville stood up to flee.

"Don't be silly, Neville." Alice-Miranda passed Millie a glass of fizzing liquid. "I'm sure it's just your dinner."

She bounced into the foyer and opened the door. A strong smell of curry drifted into the room.

"Hello." Alice-Miranda introduced herself. "I'm Alice-Miranda Highton-Smith-Kennington-Jones. And you must be Mr. Henderson. Thank you so much for bringing Neville some dinner."

"I was surprised to get the call, miss," Henderson replied. "I thought Master Neville must have eaten at the party."

"No, he wasn't feeling well, so my friend Millie and I offered to accompany him back here and stay with him for a bit," Alice-Miranda explained. "Didn't I see you yesterday up on the bridge, Mr. Henderson? With the first officer."

"Yes, miss," he replied. "He certainly likes to keep me busy." The steward entered the sitting room and placed the tray on the dining table.

"Are you all right, Master Neville?" he asked, eyeing his young charge. "Is your forehead sore?"

Neville shook his head and cast his eyes to the ground.

"If there's anything more I can do, you know how to reach me." Henderson uncovered the steaming plates. "Oh, and I found your trumpet case."

"My trumpet case?" Neville's voice quavered.

"Yes, I was surprised to see it poking out from behind a potted plant in a storeroom near the ballroom. I know how attached to it you are," Henderson explained.

Millie and Alice-Miranda shot one another a look.

"Thank you very much, Mr. Henderson," Alice-Miranda said quickly.

"Where is it?" Millie demanded.

"I put it in the bedroom under the pillow. I thought Master Neville would find it as soon as he went to bed tonight," Henderson replied. "I'll get it for you."

Henderson walked through into the bedroom. His eyes darted around at the open wardrobe doors and rumpled duvet cover, which he immediately set about straightening up.

"Sorry, it's a mess." Alice-Miranda had followed the steward into the room. "We can fix it."

"It's no bother." Henderson closed the wardrobe doors. "What were you looking for?" He pulled the trumpet case from its hiding spot under the pillows and handed it to Neville. All three of the children had joined him in the bedroom.

"Neville's trumpet case, of course," Millie said. "Weren't we, Neville?" She nudged the poor lad in the ribs.

"Yes," he murmured.

"But since you found it, we don't need to look anymore," said Alice-Miranda.

"Well, if there's nothing else, I'll be off." Henderson made a beeline for the door, muttering something to himself about having to report to the bridge again.

Millie raced out of the bedroom and retrieved Neville's case from the cupboard where it was hidden. She plonked it beside Lush's on the bed. "Gosh, it does look exactly like your case, Neville."

"Imagine that there were two young musicians out there in the world who had identical cases, and placed identical smiley-face stickers in the middle of the lid. What a strange coincidence," Alice-Miranda marveled.

"Do you r-r-really think there might be s-s-stolen jewels in there?" Neville stammered.

"Of course not," Alice-Miranda replied. But she wasn't so sure. There were certainly some odd things going on.

"Well, I think we should take a look." Millie began to fiddle with the lock on the side of Dr. Lush's case. "If Dr. Lush is responsible for all those thefts, then this is a very important discovery. Your father said that the Orlov Diamond is one of the largest in the world."

Although Alice-Miranda never liked to think the worst of anyone, she agreed that this was a mystery that had to be solved.

Millie snapped open the locks and slowly raised the lid. But there wasn't a diamond in sight.

"What's that?" Millie could barely mask her disappointment.

Alice-Miranda peered inside.

"It's an urn. Like a vase, only with a lid, and by the looks of this one, I'd say it's rather precious," Alice-Miranda replied.

Neville pointed at a gold plate on the base. "What's that?" It was engraved, but the letters were not English.

"I think it's Russian." Alice-Miranda leaned in close to have a better look. "Can you pass me a piece of paper and a pen please, Millie?"

Millie raced over to the writing desk and retrieved a notepad and pen.

Alice-Miranda set about copying the characters down.

"What are you doing?" Millie asked.

"I think I know someone who can tell us what this says," she said slowly as she concentrated on getting the letters right.

"What are we going to do about Dr. Lush and

Mr. Alex?" Neville rasped. "They're going to tell the admiral about me and then I'm going to be in trouble. And what about the bag of jewels? They must have taken them."

Alice-Miranda was silent. Things were not right on the *Octavia,* and she was determined to find out what was going on before anything could spoil her favorite aunt's wedding day.

Chapter 33

Alice-Miranda left Neville to eat his dinner and headed back upstairs to the party. She thought that her mother would be wondering where on earth she and Millie had got to. Millie offered to stay with the nervous lad and said that she could probably fend off the good doctor if he arrived at the suite. She wasn't quite sure *how,* but she would think of something. Dr. Lush's trumpet case was placed in the wardrobe and Neville's was returned to the cabinet for safekeeping.

As Alice-Miranda arrived at the ballroom, she was greeted by the sound of laughter rising above the strains of an expertly played sitar. To her delight,

Mrs. Oliver and Shilly were treating the whole room to a dance they had clearly prepared earlier.

Alice-Miranda interrupted her mother's giggling. "Hello, Mummy."

"Oh, hello there, darling. Where on earth have you been? I was beginning to worry—although I know I shouldn't. I mean, we are on a ship, and it's not as if you're likely to be kidnapped or meet any dangerous criminals now, is it? Isn't this just the most gorgeous thing you've ever seen?" Cecelia pointed toward the shimmying senior citizens, who had the entire ballroom mesmerized.

"Wow, they're very good," Alice-Miranda agreed, taking in the spectacle before her.

Lucas walked over to where Alice-Miranda was standing beside her mother. "Would you like to dance? I think we're all being instructed to take the lead from Mrs. Oliver and Shilly, and it sort of looks like fun," Lucas asked.

"Oh, hello, Lucas. Yes it certainly does." Alice-Miranda glanced around the room. "Where are Jacinta and Sep?"

"They're already out there." Lucas pointed toward Jacinta in her hot pink sari and Sep in his Nehru shirt and black trousers. "Where's Millie?"

Alice-Miranda didn't lie. "She's just keeping a friend company for a little while. She'll be back soon."

"Well, her parents seem to be enjoying themselves, that's for sure." Lucas chuckled at Pippa and Hamish, who looked as though they were having a great time keeping up with Mrs. Oliver and Ambrose, who had joined her on the dance floor. "Isn't that Jacinta's mother over there in the corner?"

"Why don't you go and join Sep and Jacinta? I don't think a partner is an absolute requirement of this type of dancing," Alice-Miranda suggested as she looked at the rows of eager participants. "I'll be there soon."

Alice-Miranda scurried toward the far corner, where Ambrosia Headlington-Bear was sitting alone, staring into the crowd. Her citrus-yellow sari looked exquisite against her tanned skin. Her huge green eyes were framed by the longest of lashes, and her makeup was perfect. An oval sapphire the size of a pigeon's egg and encircled by diamonds was lashed around her throat, held in place by five rows of lustrous pearls.

"Hello, Mrs. Headlington . . . I mean, Ambrosia." Alice-Miranda sat down in the empty chair beside her.

"Oh, hello." Ambrosia's eyes flickered toward the child.

"That's a gorgeous choker," Alice-Miranda said.

"Yes, Neville gave it to me for our anniversary. It once belonged to Catherine the Great, or so his personal assistant wrote in the note that was with it when it arrived." Ambrosia fingered the jewel.

"Neville? How do you know Neville?" Alice-Miranda asked, wide-eyed.

"He's my husband. Neville Headlington-Bear," Ambrosia sneered.

"Oh, your husband, of course." Alice-Miranda thought for a moment. "But didn't Mr. Headlington-Bear give it to you in person?"

Ambrosia made a strange sort of grunting noise. "You're kidding, aren't you? I haven't seen him in months."

"Oh." Alice-Miranda stopped, puzzled. "But he's here on the ship with you now, isn't he?"

"As far as I know, my husband is somewhere in the depths of Africa signing a deal on a mining venture or something equally dull," Ambrosia replied.

Alice-Miranda was rapidly putting the pieces together. No wonder Neville hadn't been discovered by the crew.

"Are you having a good time?" she asked.

"No, not really," Ambrosia replied tartly.

"Is there something the matter?" the child persisted.

"Well, I don't know anyone, and no one seems especially interested to know me," Ambrosia complained.

"Well, of course you know Jacinta," Alice-Miranda said gently. "And I'd be very happy to introduce you around. Although, I have to warn you that some of our distant relatives are a little bit interesting. I think eccentric is what I'd prefer to call them—but they're guaranteed to keep you amused."

"I'm fine," Ambrosia insisted. "I'll never see any of them again after we get off the ship anyway."

"Oh, I'm sure that's not the case," Alice-Miranda replied. "Jacinta and I are going to be friends forever. You and Mr. Headlington-Bear will be like part of the family."

"Family," Ambrosia scoffed. "I can't imagine."

"I can't think of anything better than family. I've always longed for brothers and sisters, but Mummy said that wasn't to be . . . . but now I've got Millie and Jacinta and Sep and Lucas and all my other friends at school, and Mrs. Oliver and Shilly and everyone at home. We might not be related by blood, but I consider them my family just the same," Alice-Miranda prattled.

"They're only using you." Ambrosia's words sliced through the air.

"I don't see what you mean," said Alice-Miranda, wrinkling her nose.

"They only like you because you're rich and you can give them things they'd never have, take them places they'd never go, give them a life they can't afford." Ambrosia's emerald eyes filled with tears.

"Is that what people do to you?" Alice-Miranda reached out and touched Ambrosia's creamy hand.

"Of course not. Don't be ridiculous." The woman withdrew her hand and wiped the moisture from her eyes. "Run along with your friends."

"Why don't you come and join us?" Alice-Miranda asked.

Ambrosia was watching her only daughter as she shimmied and shook, laughing with the two handsome lads Ambrosia had met the night before and a rather ancient gray-haired woman who was swaying wildly with a walking stick in her left hand.

"But I'll have to warn you to stay out of Granny Bert's reach—she looks rather dangerous with that stick," Alice-Miranda giggled as she surveyed the show in front of them.

"No. I'll stay here," Ambrosia protested.

Alice-Miranda tried again. "Please come. Jacinta would love to spend more time with you."

"Jacinta doesn't need me." Ambrosia stood and stalked to the other side of the room.

Alice-Miranda frowned. Grown-ups could be so complicated at times.

Chapter 34

While watching the dance floor, Alice-Miranda had come up with a plan. But Neville would have to agree, and that might prove difficult. Earlier she had promised him that she wouldn't tell anyone about him, and she'd already told Millie.

"Hello there," Alice-Miranda called above the music to Lucas, Sep and Jacinta, who were all mastering the art of the Bollywood shoulder-shrug.

"Hey!" Sep grinned. "I know we must look ridiculous but this is kind of fun."

"No, you look like experts," Alice-Miranda replied.

The music stopped and there was much clapping as the crowd scattered from the dance floor back to their seats. A swarm of white-suited drinks waiters delivered refreshments to the tables of thirsty dancers. Alice-Miranda's friends promptly downed their pitcher of iced raspberry cordial.

"Where's Millie?" Jacinta asked, looking around the room.

"Well, I need to tell you something, but you all have to promise that you won't say a word to anyone," Alice-Miranda whispered.

"That sounds mysterious." Lucas grinned—and Jacinta's heart fluttered as if filled with a thousand butterflies.

"I've made a new friend, and I want him to spend the rest of the cruise with us," said Alice-Miranda.

"Of course," Sep agreed. "Any friend of yours is a friend of ours."

"Well, it's not quite that simple . . . maybe it is. Why don't you all stay here and I'll go and get him," the tiny child instructed.

Alice-Miranda leapt from her chair and raced out of the ballroom. She flew downstairs to the Gallery Deck as fast as she could. Alice-Miranda didn't have to tell her friends Neville's story. He could just become one of the group. That would keep him out of Dr. Lush's way, and it was likely no one would notice him. He could have been any of the young boys on the ship, really. She wasn't lying—and it would only be a couple of days and Neville would be safely home again.

As she reached the door to the Albert Suite, Alice-Miranda knocked gently.

"It's me," she whispered. Millie opened the door and Alice-Miranda promptly scurried inside.

"Neville, I've got an idea," she blurted. "But you're going to have to trust me. . . ."

Millie nodded in agreement. "That's perfect. You can just hang out with us. I mean, you could be anyone. No offense, Neville."

"But how many people are on board?" Neville whispered.

"Well, including the crew, around five hundred," Alice-Miranda replied. "There are about thirty children, I think, but we seem to have divided into a few groups. Anyway, Neville, you do look a lot like some of Mummy's Swedish cousins. I'm sure that if we just keep to ourselves no one will ask too many questions."

"And what about Dr. Lush?" asked Neville. He still looked as if he might throw up.

"I'll talk to him tomorrow," Alice-Miranda promised.

"But if he really is a dangerous criminal, he might throw you overboard!" Millie gasped.

"Millie, your imagination is getting to be as good as Jacinta's," Alice-Miranda chided. "I'm glad she doesn't know about this. Can you imagine? She'd have us all marked for shark bait."

Millie giggled.

"What about Henderson?" Neville asked. "He seems to think I'm here with my mother."

"That's all right. We can let him think that for now," Alice-Miranda replied.

And so it was agreed. Neville would head up to the party with the girls and meet Sep, Lucas and Jacinta. Then Alice-Miranda would go first thing in the morning to have a chat with Dr. Lush about returning his case.

"But what if Lush comes back in the middle of the night?" Neville's face was as pale as pancake batter.

"I imagine if Aunty Gee's not feeling well, Dr. Lush will be on duty all evening. Attending to Her Majesty is no small matter."

Neville seemed slightly reassured. He'd never met anyone like Alice-Miranda before. She was so confident and organized.

"I wonder if we can find you something a little

more appropriate to wear," said Alice-Miranda with a glance at Neville's polo and trainers. "If you're going to fit in upstairs, you need to be dressed for Bollywood, and I'm afraid what you're wearing just won't do."

"Didn't your mother pack some things for the boys in your luggage just in case?" Millie asked.

Alice-Miranda clapped her hands together in delight. "Yes, I think she did."

"I'll go." Millie was already charging out the door before Alice-Miranda had time to say anything.

"I-I'm sorry about all this," Neville apologized. "I didn't mean to be a bother."

"Oh, Neville, don't be silly." Alice-Miranda smiled at him. "Think of it as an adventure."

Millie returned with the clothes. Fortunately, Neville and Sep were almost the same size, and although the white shirt was a little snug, he looked the part. Cecelia Highton-Smith had thought of everything. There was even a pair of smart black shoes. They were a little big, but Alice-Miranda improvised and stuffed the toes with toilet paper. Neville was all set.

"Come on." Alice-Miranda straightened his jacket. "You look great."

Neville grabbed his inhaler from the bedside table and took a puff.

Five minutes later the three children were upstairs in the ballroom. Alice-Miranda introduced Neville to Lucas, Sep and Jacinta. He thought they all seemed nice enough, and better still, they were too busy dancing to ask him any questions.

Chapter 35

The next morning Alice-Miranda was out of bed and dressed before dawn. She was careful not to wake her friends. Jacinta was snoring loudly and Millie's breathing was deep and even. Clutching the words she had copied from the base of the urn the night before, she knew there was at least one man on board who could translate for her—and perhaps put her mind at ease.

Neville had insisted that he would be all right sleeping in his suite. Millie said he should prop a chair under the door handle for extra security, and that was exactly what he had done. Considering the drama of the day, Neville had quickly fallen into a deep sleep and was roused by the beeping of his bed-side alarm, which he'd set for six a.m. He wanted to be up before Henderson arrived—or worse.

The children had arranged to meet in the library at eight a.m. and go to breakfast together. Although Jacinta, Sep and Lucas were not fully aware of the situation with Neville, Alice-Miranda had decided there'd be safety in numbers; if Dr. Lush saw Neville among the children, he'd be less likely to make a scene. Or so she hoped.

Alice-Miranda left the suite and made her way downstairs toward the kitchen. The ship was ghostly quiet at that hour, and she was pleased not to run into anyone on the way.

Through the plastic doorway at the end of the hall she could see several chefs already busy at work.

"Hello." Her tiny voice floated into the stainless-steel room. "Good morning, Chef Vladimir."

The Russian giant tensed at the sound of the child's voice.

"What now?" he hissed through gritted teeth.

Alice-Miranda rounded the corner into the main section of the kitchen. Vladimir had been attending to the day's menu when she interrupted his train of thought. "Hello, Chef Vladimir. Thank you for sending that delicious room service last night. My friend adored your chicken curry. Did you get to see any of the dancing? It was such a fun night, don't you think?" She looked up at him with her huge brown eyes.

"What you want? I am busy man," Vladimir growled.

"Oh yes, Chef Vladimir. I know you are. That's why I came so early . . . ," Alice-Miranda began.

"You think this is early? I have been here since three," Vladimir replied, narrowing his eyes.

"Goodness, you must get by on hardly any sleep at all. I need at least eight hours or I'm a mess," said Alice-Miranda.

"Well, what you want?" Vladimir demanded. "I don't have time to waste, and you are biggest time waster on ship."

"Well, I came to ask you about this." Alice-Miranda produced a folded piece of paper from her jacket pocket. "I wondered if you would be so kind as to translate it for me? I'm afraid I don't know Russian at all."

Vladimir reached out his giant paw and snatched the paper from Alice-Miranda's tiny hand. He studied it carefully.

"Where you see this?" he asked.

"On a plaque at the base of a beautiful china urn,"

Alice-Miranda replied. "I'm certain it must be very expensive."

"Then makes sense," he said.

"Please, Chef Vladimir." Alice-Miranda's eyes were wide. "Can you tell me what it says?"

"'Maria Bella Lushkov, our dearest mother.'"

"Oh." Alice-Miranda gasped and clutched her face in her hands. "Goodness. I had wondered, but I didn't like to think it could be . . . that. No wonder Dr. Lush was so upset. Thank you, Chef Vladimir. Thank you very much."

Alice-Miranda turned and scurried toward the door, intent on finding Dr. Lush immediately.

"Hey," Vladimir called after her. "Don't you want to know who she was?"

The child stopped in her tracks. She swiveled around and scampered back toward the chef.

"Did you know her?" Alice-Miranda asked, her eyes even wider than they had been a moment ago.

"In Russia, everyone know her," Vladimir replied.

Chapter 36

There was no time to lose. Alice-Miranda had listened to Chef Vladimir's story, and it seemed Maria Bella Lushkov had been very famous indeed. She hurried back along the dimly lit corridors to the Albert Suite.

Neville leapt when Alice-Miranda rapped sharply at the door.

"It's me, Neville," she whispered.

The door opened slightly. Neville poked his head around just to be sure and then ushered her inside.

"Where's Dr. Lush's case?" Alice-Miranda puffed.

"Please, may I have it? I've worked out what's inside it and I need to take it to him immediately."

Neville didn't like the sound of this. "What is it?"

"Well, this is going to sound odd, but I think it's his mother," she replied as Neville retrieved the battered case from where he had hidden it in the wardrobe.

"What?" The boy dropped it to the floor.

"Oh dear, I hope it didn't break." Alice-Miranda bit her lip. "That would be terrible."

"Wh-wh-wh-hat do you mean it's his m-m-mother?" Neville looked as if he was about to faint.

Alice-Miranda picked the case up and placed it carefully onto the dining table. She gently pried open the locks, and to her great relief the urn was still in one piece. "Well, that nameplate says 'Maria Bella Lushkov, our dearest mother.'" She pointed at the engraving in all its Russian code.

"How do you know?"

"Remember, I copied it down yesterday and this morning a friend translated it for me. And don't you remember that Admiral Harding said that Mr. Alex's name was Lushkov? I wouldn't mind betting that Dr. Lush's name is that too but he's dropped the 'kov' for some reason or other. Lots of people with foreign-sounding names do that. I think it's a lovely name, but he must have his reasons. So I'm sure they probably *are* brothers. Anyway, if this is Dr. Lush's mother's ashes, then it's no wonder he's upset about losing her."

"Ashes?" Neville gulped. "But why would he bring them on the ship?"

"I don't know, really. That's a bit of a mystery, but everything else makes sense, doesn't it? When he was saying that they'd brought her all the way from Russia and she was the most precious thing in the world. Except, I don't know why they would have said they'd be in terrible trouble if anything happened to her. I think something already has," Alice-Miranda declared.

"What are you going to do?" Neville didn't like the thought of having a dead woman's ashes in his cabin one bit.

"I'm going to take the case and find Dr. Lush right this minute. I'm sure that if I explain your situation he won't make a fuss."

Neville's face drained of color. "But he said that he'd tell the admiral."

"Look, Neville, I suspect Dr. Lush will be so glad to have his case back that he'll be quite happy to keep our secret for the next couple of days. It's hardly as though you're a dangerous criminal, is it? Goodness, I think we might even be able to have some fun— and you'll get to come to the wedding too." Alice-Miranda's eyes twinkled.

"What about that bag of jewels?" After Neville had returned to his suite last night, he had searched high and low to see if he could find it.

Alice-Miranda closed the lid of the case.

"Didn't you hit your head yesterday morning? Do you think that perhaps you imagined that you'd found them, or you dreamt it?" Alice-Miranda was trying to find a rational explanation.

"I don't think so." Neville looked glum. "I don't know. Maybe."

After tearing the place apart, he'd begun to doubt himself too.

"Maybe it was the shock of everything," suggested Alice-Miranda.

The boy shrugged. Alice-Miranda reached out and placed her hands firmly on Neville's shoulders. "I'm sure that once I return the case to Dr. Lush, everything will work out just fine."

Neville wasn't entirely convinced, but he had come to realize that if anyone knew what she was doing, it was this little girl.

"D-d-do you want me to come with you?" Neville

offered. He was attempting to be valiant but rather hoped that she'd refuse his offer.

"No, I'll be fine. Just meet everyone at the library at eight. I'll see you there."

Alice-Miranda picked up Dr. Lush's case and left the room. Although she dearly hoped that returning the case would put everything to rights, she couldn't shake the feeling that Neville hadn't imagined that laundry bag full of jewels. Something else was going on too. She just had to work out what it was.

Chapter 37

Alice-Miranda navigated her way to Dr. Lush's office. It was now quarter past seven, and she wondered if he might not yet be in. As luck would have it, the doctor was just returning from his night-long vigil with Her Majesty. It was common knowledge that the Queen suffered from an acute allergy to crustaceans; hence they were never served on any of her menus. When Nicholas had reached her suite last evening, he'd found Queen Georgiana particularly wheezy and had immediately administered a shot of adrenaline and some steroids. After his encounter with Admiral Harding, there was no way he was going to leave the room until Her Majesty was fully recovered. Dead monarchs were not something he was prepared to have on his conscience.

Lush traipsed toward his office. Dark circles hung beneath his eyes, and he yawned loudly as he reached the door.

"Good morning, Dr. Lush." Alice-Miranda bounced toward him.

"Oh godfathers," he muttered. "Not you again. What is it this time? A hangnail?" He put his key in the door. "Well?" He glanced over his shoulder through squinty eyes.

Alice-Miranda followed him into the waiting room holding the trumpet case firmly in her right hand. "No, I'm perfectly fine," she announced. "I just need to talk to you about something."

Dr. Lush opened the internal surgery door and walked through. She heard the computer whir as he jiggled the mouse to wake it up.

"What is it, then?" he called. "Come on. I haven't got all day."

The tiny girl pushed open the door, strode to the chair beside the doctor's desk and scrambled onto it. She placed the battered case on her lap.

Nicholas was preoccupied with the computer and hadn't taken any notice.

"Dr. Lush," Alice-Miranda said. "I've found something that I think belongs to you, or to Mr. Alex."

"What?" He glanced toward her at last. "Mummy!" he gasped as he caught sight of the case. Dr. Lush snatched it up and put it on his desk, sprang the locks and opened the lid. He reached out and picked up the urn, then held it tightly to his chest. A tear glistened in the doctor's eye. Alice-Miranda reached across the desk and offered him a tissue, which he promptly snatched.

"Where did you get this?" His voice quavered.

"Well, it's quite a long story, Dr. Lush. And one that will surely put your mind at ease about Neville," Alice-Miranda began. "Why don't you sit there and I'll make us both a nice cup of tea."

Alice-Miranda had noticed the day before, while waiting for her splinter to be removed, that there was a small kitchenette off the side of the consulting room. She dashed inside and busied herself making Dr. Lush a brew.

"Why don't you telephone Mr. Alex?" the child called while she poured the tea. "Perhaps he'd like to come and hear what happened too."

"What? How do you know about him?" Dr. Lush glared at Alice-Miranda as she placed a teacup and saucer in front of him.

"That's not important, Dr. Lush. But I'm sure he'll be pleased to know that the case has been returned."

Alexander Lushkov arrived not long after Nicholas summoned him. Together the pair listened to Alice-Miranda and her fanciful tale about Neville Nordstrom and the two trumpet cases.

"He's terribly scared of being in trouble with his parents," Alice-Miranda explained. "After everything the poor boy's been through, it would be lovely if he could just enjoy himself until we dock."

Nicholas and Alexander exchanged knowing looks.

"Seeing she's been so honest, I think we should tell her our story too," Alexander said. The doctor gave a small nod.

"Please, I'm a very good listener," Alice-Miranda offered.

"Maria Bella, she was our beloved mother," Dr. Lush began.

"And she was beloved by all of Russia too," Alex added.

"Your mother was famous," Alice-Miranda said.

"It all began a long time ago when we were just small boys. Our mother had the voice of an angel. She loved to sing, but she sang only for us and our father," Dr. Lush said.

"But then our papa . . ." Alex sniffed.

"Are you all right, Mr. Alex?" Alice-Miranda popped up and snatched a tissue from the box on Dr. Lush's desk and handed it to him.

"One morning on his way to work, our papa suffered a massive heart attack," Dr. Lush continued, "and passed away."

"Oh, that's terrible!" Alice-Miranda clasped her hands together tightly.

"And we had no money, so our mother worked many hours, all day and half the night. She took in ironing and sewing and she looked after children and cooked. She wore herself out, but all the time she sang. She said that she was singing our father home," Alex said.

"That's so beautiful." Alice-Miranda looked up at the brothers, wide-eyed.

"And then one day a man passing beneath the open window heard her singing. He was the director of the St. Petersburg Opera and could recognize a great talent when he heard it," Alex explained.

"Our mother, Maria Bella Lushkov, soon became the most celebrated star of the Russian opera, renowned across the world for her soprano voice," Dr. Lush added.

"Mama got sick a little while ago, and on her deathbed, she asked that we take her home to Venice, where our grandfather had taught her to sing," Alex explained.

"Well, of course you should do that," Alice-Miranda agreed. "But I don't understand why you didn't just take a flight and go to Venice."

"It's because of her fame. She is a national treasure, and the authorities would not allow such a thing. We had to steal her from the crypt, and when I heard that the *Octavia* was heading for Venice and this was a top-secret cruise, I thought it was perfect. I got Alex a job in the band so we could do this together," Dr. Lush added.

"That's a wonderful story," said Alice-Miranda. She walked over to the two men and patted each one on the hand.

"Thank you for finding her." Alex smiled. "We appreciate it."

"Yes, thank you, Alice-Miranda. Perhaps I have been wrong about children," Dr. Lush added. "Well, some children."

Alice-Miranda smiled at the brothers. "I'm just glad that things have worked out."

Chapter 38

Alice-Miranda met her friends as planned in the library right at eight a.m. Her beaming smile gave Neville great comfort, as did her emphatic wink.

"So, where did you disappear to this morning?" Millie whispered as the children made their way to the breakfast room.

"I'll tell you all about it later," Alice-Miranda whispered back. "But everything is fine with Neville and Dr. Lush. Dr. Lush has his case, and he said that as long as I can vouch for Neville he won't tell anyone about him."

"That's fantastic." Millie squeezed her friend's hand.

Jacinta caught up to them. "What are you two talking about?"

"I was just saying that I think we should work out what we're going to do today. We won't be able to play much at all tomorrow."

"Why not?" Jacinta asked.

"Because it's the wedding," Lucas reminded her. "Have you forgotten why we're here? I was hoping you'd save me a dance." He winked.

All Jacinta could do was sigh.

Alice-Miranda and Millie chuckled.

Over the most delicious breakfast of scrambled eggs, crispy bacon, tropical fruits, tea and toast, the group decided that they would spend the morning playing some games on deck, probably take a swim (Neville didn't mention that he didn't have any trunks with him and would prefer to sit that one out) and then they'd take in a film in the small theater. That night Lawrence and Charlotte were hosting a formal dinner in honor of Aunty Gee to thank her for allowing them to have the wedding on board the *Octavia*.

Alice-Miranda made sure that Neville sat between her and Millie at breakfast and managed to deflect questions from the other children that meant disclosing any details about Neville and his family. It helped that Alice-Miranda had also told the group the night before that he was painfully shy and found talking quite an ordeal.

The children had almost finished their meal when the room began to fill with adults busily laughing and recalling the previous evening's festivities— particularly Shilly and Mrs. Oliver's spectacular dance moves. Alice-Miranda had greeted her parents, who were surprised to see her and the other children up and about so early. Millie had a quick catch-up with her mum and dad, but Ambrosia Headlington-Bear was nowhere to be seen. Charlotte and Lawrence arrived and were quickly surrounded by friends. Alice-Miranda was beginning to wonder if she would have any time at all with her aunt before the end of the cruise.

"Who's that blond boy over there with your friends?" Cecelia asked as she waved at the group sitting several tables away.

"That's Neville," Alice-Miranda replied.

"Who does he belong to?" she asked, then said, "Oh goodness, with hair that color he must be Cousin Alfred's youngest. Hasn't he grown?"

Alice-Miranda didn't correct her mother.

"We'll see you later, Mummy." She kissed her mother's cheek. "Bye, Daddy." Alice-Miranda gave her father a tight squeeze.

As the children were leaving, Lady Sarah and Lord Robert arrived with their daughters Annie and Poppy in tow.

"Good morning," Alice-Miranda greeted her cousins.

"Hello there, young lady." Lord Robert offered a tight smile. "Lovely party last night, wasn't it?"

"Oh yes, lots of fun. That's a gorgeous hat, Lady Sarah," Alice-Miranda commented, taking in the oversized black-and-white polka-dot panama.

Sarah's face was pinched into a grimace. "Thank you, sweetheart," she replied.

"You know, you look different this morning." Alice-Miranda studied her mother's cousin, trying to work it out. It couldn't have been her hair. It was hidden beneath the hat. And she certainly hadn't gained weight. And then it hit her like a lightning bolt. "I know. You're not wearing any jewelry. Well, not much, anyway."

Tears welled in Lady Sarah's eyes.

"Alice-Miranda's right, Mummy," said Annie. She gazed up at her mother. "Where are your necklaces and your bangles?"

"I decided to try a new look, that's all." Lady Sarah wiped her forefinger across the corner of her eye.

"Well, I think you look lovely, with or without your jewels." Alice-Miranda smiled.

The Adamses moved inside. Alice-Miranda's mind was ticking. Lady Sarah was always the most bejeweled of her relatives. Some days she wore an armful of gold bracelets, and she was never shy of mixing her pearls with long gold chains or other expensive trinkets. Her mummy said that before the girls were even teenagers, her cousin Sarah had amassed an impressive collection of glitter. Everyone knew it was her thing. And now, apart from her gold watch, she was practically naked. Something about that picture was very wrong indeed.

Chapter 39

illie and Neville exchanged looks as the group
headed off to the Promenade Deck for some
games. While the boys and Jacinta were organizing
the chess pieces on the giant board, Millie took the
opportunity to have a quiet word with Alice-Miranda.

"I heard what you said to Lady Sarah about her
jewelry. Do you think that bag Neville found could
have been hers?"

"I'm not sure, but it does seem a very strange coincidence," Alice-Miranda replied. "But it's not in the
suite anymore, so we can't prove anything."

"If they'd been robbed, surely they would have reported it to Admiral Harding," Millie said.

"Yes, I'm sure they would have." Alice-Miranda nodded thoughtfully.

"Come on," Sep called. "We're going to play in teams. Neville, me and Millie against Alice-Miranda, Jacinta and Lucas."

"Coming!" the girls chorused.

The morning flew by. Neville proved to be a chess champion. He knew all the moves, and his team won the tournament three games to two. He still didn't say much, but he seemed to be enjoying himself. At least he hadn't scurried back to his room.

Just before eleven a.m., Charlotte arrived on deck.

"Hello, miss." Charlotte had crept up behind her niece and covered her eyes.

"Aunt Charlotte!" The tiny child spun around and was immediately scooped into Charlotte's arms. Alice-Miranda peppered her face with kisses in the usual way, before being deposited back onto the deck.

"Hello, everyone," Charlotte greeted the rest of the group. "Lawrence and I have been rather busy entertaining everyone and realized that we've spent no time with you at all. So we've arranged something rather special." Charlotte was wide-eyed.

"What is it?" Millie demanded.

"It's a surprise," Charlotte replied, raising her eyebrows. "So you'll just have to wait."

She instructed the children to follow her. Neville thought he might slip away back to his suite, but Alice-Miranda convinced him to stick with the group.

Charlotte led the way toward the rear of the ship. She descended a staircase which passed through several floors, including the Gallery Deck, right to the bottom. Alice-Miranda realized they must have been at the very back of the engine room. Her aunt pushed open a huge metal door and the children found themselves in a kind of dock area.

"There's a hole in the ship!" Jacinta exclaimed. "Are we sinking?"

Neville gulped. He'd come this far only to have the *Titanic* moment he'd been dreading after all.

"No, of course we're not sinking. The *Octavia* has its own internal dock where the mail boat comes in and where we get to take that baby out." Charlotte pointed at a rubber boat with six rows of seats and a huge engine on the back, bobbing alongside the ship.

"Hello, you lot." In his seat beside the driver, Lawrence was grinning from ear to ear. "Come on, what are you waiting for?"

A row of orange life jackets hung along the wall. The children took no time at all getting them on, then hopped into the boat and buckled up. Apparently Aunty Gee had decided a little while ago that she needed something for the younger guests to entertain themselves with, and so this little jet boat had been a recent addition. There was another smaller speedboat hanging on a rigging inside the dock too.

The outboard motor sputtered into life and a plume of smoke rose up from the rear of the boat as the driver revved the engine. Lawrence turned around and waved. "Okay, everyone, hold on!"

Jacinta had a viselike grip on the bar in front of her. "Is this sa-a-a-afe?" Her voice drifted on the breeze as the boat roared away from the ship, thumping over the small waves. Her question was drowned out by the children's hysterical laughter.

When the driver held his right hand aloft and made a circle in the air, the boat suddenly spun a full 360 degrees.

Water sprayed all over the passengers, but Jacinta seemed to be sitting in the worst possible spot. She was wet through.

"Argh! I'm drowned!" Jacinta squealed.

"This is the best!" Millie yelled above the noise.

Neville got the hiccups.

Alice-Miranda was sitting beside him. "You poor thing," she laughed. Neville just smiled, then hiccupped again.

The boat sped around the ship, its outboard motor

buzzing like a baritone bee. The noise had garnered some attention from the passengers, and when Cecelia and Hugh spotted the children, they waved madly from the upper deck.

Aunty Gee and Granny Valentina were taking an early lunch in the smaller dining room and could see the boat zipping to and fro.

"That does look good fun." Granny Valentina took a sip of tea.

"Yes, what's say you and I give it a go tomorrow morning, dear?" Aunty Gee arched her left eyebrow.

"But, ma'am, if I may," Mrs. Marmalade began. "I don't think that's a very sensible idea."

"Oh, Mrs. Marmalade, sensible is terribly overrated—wouldn't you agree, Valentina?" Aunty Gee winked.

Mrs. Marmalade excused herself from the luncheon table and scurried away to find Dalton to see if he couldn't talk sense into Her Majesty.

Half an hour later, after the jet boat had made more 360-degree turns than anyone could remember and the laughter had dulled from squeals and shrieks to giggles, the boat motored slowly back to the retractable pontoon beside the ship. The children were all trembling from laughter and exhilaration.

"That was awesome, Dad." Lucas couldn't stop

smiling as he and his father walked side by side back into the cavernous dock area.

"Thanks . . . that was amazing . . . fantastic . . . the best," the children chorused.

"Our pleasure." Charlotte smiled. "We hoped you'd enjoy it."

"What are you doing after lunch?" Lawrence asked the group once they were all safely back inside the ship.

"I'm going to the movies," Jacinta declared. "I heard there's a fantastic new film screening called *Paris,* starring some rather handsome fellow. I think his name's Lawrence Ridley," she finished with a wink.

The children laughed.

Neville hadn't expected to enjoy himself quite so much at all. His hiccups had lasted the entire time but stopped once he was back on board.

"Did you have fun?" Alice-Miranda asked as she walked alongside him.

"Yes." He nodded.

"Isn't this amazing?" Alice-Miranda looked around at all the pulleys and cables.

"Astonishing," Neville replied. "I would never have guessed you could have all this on a ship."

The children returned to the dining room for a bite of lunch before heading to the little theater. The weather had turned decidedly gray, and several of the passengers were already fretting about the possibility of another storm.

Admiral Harding seemed to spend most of his time pacing the ship.

"Gosh, the admiral is in a funny mood," Lucas said when the old man passed them for the fifth time just after lunch and asked them for the fifth time if they were all right.

"He looks like he's expecting something terrible to happen," Jacinta added. "Like there's a bomb on board or we're about to get taken over by pirates."

"Jacinta!" the group chided in unison.

"You know, after you win your gold medal at the Olympics, you should definitely become a newsreader," Sep added.

"Why?" she asked.

"Because you love being the bearer of bad news," he said, and the group laughed.

Jacinta rolled her eyes and poked out her tongue.

It seemed that word had spread of the screening, and there was nothing could fill a theater as fast as bad weather and a gorgeous movie star. By the time the show was ready to start, almost every one of the three hundred seats was full.

As the lights dimmed, Granny Bert could be heard loudly requesting that one of the stewards bring her a chocolate-dipped ice cream swirl, while the children munched their popcorn and sat back to enjoy the film.

An hour and three quarters later the audience was clapping and cheering and in some cases bawling their eyes out. Shilly and Mrs. Oliver were both reaching for their handkerchiefs, Granny Bert was telling Daisy that she should marry that gorgeous fellow, Lawrence Ridley, completely forgetting that they were on the ship for his wedding to Charlotte, and Jacinta just seemed lost in a trance.

"That was wonderful," she gushed. "Your father is the most amazing actor."

"Yeah, he's pretty good," Lucas agreed. "He always seems to get the girl."

"And save the day." Sep grinned.

As they were leaving the theater, the children ran into Alice-Miranda's mother.

"Did you enjoy that?" Cecelia inquired.

"Oh yes, Mummy, it was wonderful," Alice-Miranda replied. "Isn't Uncle Lawrence clever? He should win an Academy Award for that one."

"Oooh yes!" Jacinta was bug-eyed. "I'd be so proud."

Everyone hooted with laughter.

"You'll need to go and start getting ready for dinner soon. It's formal. Think of it as practice for tomorrow," Cecelia advised.

As the children headed for their suites, Alice-Miranda walked alongside Neville. "I don't suppose you have a dinner suit among your things?" she whispered.

Neville shook his head. "It's okay. I'd rather stay in."

"Don't be silly," Alice-Miranda reassured him. "I'm sure we can arrange something. Besides, if you stay in you'll only worry about things."

"How did you know?" Neville almost managed a smile.

"Did you enjoy yourself today?" Alice-Miranda asked.

Neville nodded. "I haven't even thought about, you know . . ."

"Well, then you must come to the party tonight!" Alice-Miranda said, and waved goodbye to Neville as he headed downstairs to the Gallery Deck.

"Bye, Neville!" the group chorused. "See you later."

Neville blushed, before his whole face crumpled upward into a smile.

Chapter 40

Sloane Sykes arrived home from school to find her mother standing at the kitchen sink drumming her red talons on the granite benchtop like a slow march, over and over again.

"Hello, Mummy." Sloane threw her backpack into the corner. "I need a drink."

When her mother didn't move, Sloane opened the fridge and took out a two-liter bottle of diet cola. She proceeded to pour herself an enormous glass, then sat down at the bench to consume it. Her mother hadn't turned around at all and seemed rather lost in her thoughts.

Sloane was preoccupied too. Her day had begun

with a slew of taunts from Lola, a brunette beauty who had the whole school wrapped around her manicured pinkie nail, and had ended the same way. For whatever reason, the girl and her posse of friends had taken an intense dislike to Sloane, and whenever they saw her they called her names—in Spanish, of course, which she didn't understand, but she knew from the howls of laughter that accompanied them that they must have been unkind at the very least. Sloane had yet to make a friend and frequently found herself thinking about Alice-Miranda and Winchesterfield-Downsfordvale Academy for Proper Young Ladies. Maybe it hadn't been so bad there after all.

"Sloane," said her mother, finally spinning around to face her. "When were you going to tell me about this?" She held aloft what appeared to be a letter.

"What is it?" Sloane looked up from her half-empty glass. A gnawing feeling in her stomach told her exactly what it was, but she didn't want her mother to know she had been expecting it.

"And these?" September Sykes produced a small bundle of letters from under her latest edition of *Gloss and Goss*.

"Where did you get those? Have you been snooping in my room?" Sloane demanded.

"Have you been writing to her? That little monster who ruined all of Mummy's plans?" September stamped her foot on the tiled floor like a tantrum-throwing flamenco dancer.

"No, Mummy, I have not been writing to her," Sloane replied. "But what if I had? It's none of your business."

"None of my business?" September marched over to where Sloane was sitting and hovered above her on the other side of the island bench. "If it wasn't for Alice-Miranda or whatever her stupid name is, we'd be living the high life now."

"And what do you call this, Mummy?" Sloane glanced around the villa with its state-of-the-art kitchen, swimming pool and home theater. "I wouldn't exactly say that you're living rough."

"How dare you, Sloane Sykes?" September trembled like a giant butterscotch soufflé. "Your father's so busy I hardly ever get to see him, and it's not that easy making friends here when they don't even speak English."

"They don't speak English, or you don't speak Spanish? Don't talk to me about it being tough, Mother. Try going to school every day with the lovely Lola. She hates me and I don't even know why," Sloane spat. "And you can give me my mail, thanks very much." Sloane snatched the letters from her mother's hand and raced off to the safety of the front porch.

"Urgh!" September cried, pouting. "Life still isn't fair!"

Sloane sat down on the top step. A giant skink poked his head out from under a terra-cotta pot beside her and then retreated upon spying the giant intruder.

"Don't leave," Sloane begged the frightened creature. "If you stay *she* won't come out here." She glanced over her shoulder toward the front door. Sloane placed the bundle of letters she had already read beside her. This new envelope wasn't the same as the other ones. There was no embossed AMHSKJ. This envelope was stark white, expensive-looking just the same, but bore the name *"Octavia"* in raised print on the back flap. Sloane wondered what it meant.

Dear Sloane,

I hope this letter finds you well and enjoying school. I know that the holidays are a little different for you, so I suspect that you're still in term. As you know, we're away for Aunt Charlotte's wedding. It's going to be lovely, I'm sure, but I'm writing to you because something has happened and I need your assistance. I wouldn't ask except that this is very important and a young boy's well-being depends on your help. It's not life-and-death, but I do know that his parents will be very worried and really there's no need because he's safe and sound with us. I can't say exactly where we are because we had to promise not to tell anyone. If you look inside the envelope you'll see that there's another letter addressed to Mr. and Mrs. L. Nordstrom. I believe that they live quite close to you—just down the road, in fact. Their son, Neville, has got into a bit of a tight spot, and if you could just deliver the letter and tell them that what's in it is the absolute truth, I would be most appreciative—as would my new friend, Neville. He's a delightful fellow, but quite the most nervous boy I've ever met. I know that with your help we can have all of this sorted and then Neville will be home again by the weekend. Please, Sloane, I'm relying on you. This is what I need you to do. . . .

Sloane read the letter twice. She could hardly believe what she was seeing. Alice-Miranda was asking for her help. Her first instinct was to throw the whole lot in the bin. But there was something stopping her. Sloane didn't like being hated. She wondered what it would feel like to help someone else, for no reason other than they had asked. Really, there was nothing in it for her, and yet she thought, how hard would it be to go and pay these people a visit, give them the letter, and tell them what Alice-Miranda said?

The skink poked its head out again from under the pot.

"What do you think?" Sloane addressed her reptilian companion. "Should I do it?"

The skink took another step into the sunlight. Sloane looked at him, with his giant eyes and funny earless head. And then the creature moved its head up and down. "Oh really," Sloane chuckled. "So you think I should go, do you?" The skink scuttled off back to its hiding spot. "All right then, I will."

She stood up and walked back inside to where her mother had retreated to the family room off the kitchen and was now watching her favorite game show, *Winners Are Grinners.*

"Sloane, is that you?" September said sulkily.

Sloane approached her mother slowly. "Mummy, I'm going to visit a friend."

"Good, I'm glad you've made some friends." Her mother didn't look up from the television, where the contestant was being asked, "What's the name of Queen Georgiana's royal yacht?" The program was dubbed in Spanish and had subtitles in English.

"This is so stupid," September griped. "I don't see why they couldn't just leave it in English and have the subtitles in Spanish. It takes a lot of effort to keep up with reading all those lines."

Sloane glanced at the television set as three options were given for the correct answer.

a. *Ondine*

b. *Octavia*

c. *Oriana*

Sloane's mind went into overdrive. She turned the envelope over in her hand.

"That's it. That's where they are," she whispered.

"Who? Who's where?" her mother snapped.

"No one, Mummy." Sloane smiled to herself. And with that she raced off out the front door.

Chapter 41

At exactly five minutes to seven, Jacinta and Millie met Sep and Lucas at the entrance to the ballroom. Last night's subcontinental sounds had been replaced by the smooth jazz tones of Mr. Morrison's big band. Alice-Miranda had gone downstairs to escort Neville. Upon returning to her suite earlier in the afternoon she'd had a quiet word with Mr. Winterstone, who, it seemed, could arrange many things. When Alice-Miranda knocked at the door of the Albert Suite, Neville greeted her looking resplendent in his black suit, white shirt and bow tie.

"Very handsome, Neville!" exclaimed Alice-Miranda, smiling at her new friend.

"Th-th-thank you," the boy replied as they walked upstairs. Alice-Miranda looped her arm through Neville's, and for a moment, he thought he might faint. They arrived at the ballroom at seven on the dot.

Alice-Miranda was surprised to see the room almost empty apart from Lord Robert, Lady Sarah and their girls, Millie's parents, Granny Bert, Daisy, the Greenings, Max and Cyril.

She spied Dr. Lush talking to his brother over by the band and promptly left Neville with Millie and took herself off to say hello. Alexander and Nicholas were rather more friendly toward Alice-Miranda that evening. Alex kept his earphones out for the entire conversation, and Nicholas even smiled, although he did cast a dubious look at Neville.

Aunty Gee had begun to wonder too. She was waiting in the drawing room for word that everyone had arrived before making her official entrance. She was sure the invitation had said seven p.m. and it was now almost half-past.

When Alice-Miranda returned to her friends, they found their table and sat down to have some lemonade. Mr. Winterstone was a man of many talents and had also arranged an extra place for Neville.

Enormous silver candelabra adorned each of the tables. There were floral displays in autumn hues of orange and red positioned on plinths around the glittering room.

When finally the guests began to arrive in earnest, Jacinta and Millie couldn't help but stare at the kaleidoscope of gowns and impeccably groomed ladies who wore them.

Alice-Miranda scanned the room. Her mother and father had arrived. Her mother was wearing a stunning navy gown, and her father looked terribly handsome in his dinner suit.

Cecelia saw the children pointing at her and hurried toward their table.

"Hello, Mummy. You look beautiful." Alice-Miranda leapt from her seat to give her mother a kiss.

"Oh, darling, there you are. Are you all right? Is everyone all right?" Cecelia drew her lips together in a tight line.

"Of course, Mummy. We're fine, aren't we?" Alice-Miranda asked her friends.

"Yes . . . lovely, thank you . . . great," the group replied.

Her father looked as though he was far, far away.

Alice-Miranda pulled at his sleeve. "Are you okay, Daddy?"

"What's that, darling?" Hugh looked down at his only child.

"Are you okay?" she repeated.

"Yes, of course," he replied.

But Alice-Miranda wasn't convinced. Most of the adults were acting very strangely, as though they were all chewing over a particularly tricky long-division sum and had no idea of the answer.

On the other side of the room, Dalton poked his head around the corner of the doorway and whispered to Aunty Gee, "Ma'am, I think we're ready."

A hail of trumpets announced the arrival of Queen Georgiana. Her buttercup-yellow gown fell softly from her hips into folds of organza, while the bodice was beaded in crystals. Around her neck, a diamond-encrusted choker with sapphires glinted in the soft light, and a matching sapphire tiara adorned her perfectly coiffed hair.

"Doesn't your Aunty Gee look grand?" Jacinta leaned over and whispered to Alice-Miranda. "Those jewels are something else."

And right then Alice-Miranda worked out exactly what the matter was.

Queen Georgiana reached the head table and addressed the subdued crowd.

"Good evening, everyone, and I must say that you are all looking rather splendid. Charlotte and her handsome prince, Lawrence, have arranged this party in my honor, and I would like to thank them. It is a pleasure to be hosting their wedding tomorrow.

"May I propose a toast to Charlotte and Lawrence." The Queen raised her glass.

"Charlotte and Lawrence!" reverberated around the room.

Alice-Miranda's eyes scanned the guests. Apart from Aunty Gee, none of the ladies was wearing any jewels. It was like a silent conspiracy.

"Have you seen your mother?" Millie whispered to Jacinta.

"No," she replied.

Just as Jacinta spoke, the ballroom doors burst open. There, in a fire-engine-red gown, her face streaked with tears, stood Ambrosia Headlington-Bear.

"I've been robbed!" she cried. "My jewels. They're all gone!"

The woman was near hysterical. Dalton moved swiftly to shut the doors and take the screaming woman a medicinal brandy.

Around the room, guests were glancing at one another and then reaching into their pockets and purses, fingering the notes that had replaced the jewelry in their suite safes.

Admiral Harding cleared his throat to address

the crowd. His voice trembled as he spoke. "Mrs. Headlington-Bear, I'm afraid you have put us all in grave danger with that outburst. I suspect that we have all received the same note." He pulled the paper from his pocket. "And furthermore, I suspect that you didn't bother to read yours."

White notes appeared all over the ballroom. Aunty Gee furrowed her brow. She couldn't understand why no one had informed her of what was going on. She held her hand out toward the admiral, who passed her the note. At once her expression changed. "A bomb on board the ship? Really?"

"I'm not sure who is responsible for this, but I can tell you that, once caught, he or she will feel the full force of the law," the admiral assured his guests.

"But what about the kidnappers?" Lady Sarah shouted.

"What kidnappers?" asked Cecelia, puzzled. "My note says that if I tell anyone, Alice-Miranda will be thrown overboard to the sharks."

"Well, this one says that they'll set fire to the ship," Cousin Harriet said.

"And this one says that they'll kill my darling Peppy," an elderly woman with purple hair called out.

"Who's Peppy?" Lawrence asked.

"My baby." The woman began to blubber loudly.

Lawrence gave her a quizzical look.

"My West Highland Terrier, man," the woman snapped.

"Well," Queen Georgiana said. "It sounds to me as if we're all being taken for a ride. I don't think whoever is responsible for this could possibly undertake *all* of the dastardly deeds you've just catalogued. "So"—she looked at Dalton—"do you have any ideas?"

Admiral Harding spoke up. "I need you all to calm down. Please sit." A momentary hush descended over the room.

"It must be the same gang that has been stealing all the Russian jewels," an elderly gentleman called from the far corner.

"My sapphire was worn by Catherine the Great," Ambrosia sniveled.

"That new chef's Russian. Strange coincidence that your Mr. Rodgers was taken out by a hit-and-run just before this bloke turned up," Ambrose McLoughlin-McTavish pondered loudly.

"What about you, Lushkov?" Harry Morrison, the bandleader, pointed at the wild-haired saxophonist. "You've been acting very strangely since we came on board."

The room erupted as accusations pinged from wall to wall like bullets.

Alice-Miranda beckoned to her friends to lean in close.

"They're all wrong. Chef Vladimir isn't a thief. And we know it's not Mr. Alex or Dr. Lush. Come on, let's get out of here," she instructed her friends. "We need to go somewhere quiet and think this through properly."

With the commotion raging around them, the children hurried from the ballroom.

"The library," Lucas instructed as they scurried upstairs.

The children entered what had become their own private sanctuary and Sep quickly locked the door. Neville was paler than uncooked pastry, and Jacinta was furious about her mother's outburst.

"They're all jumping to conclusions," Alice-Miranda soothed. "We need to think about the facts. Whoever's behind all this has stolen a large amount of jewelry, so I don't think they're working alone."

"Who had a key to my room?" Neville asked.

"Who had a key to *all* the rooms?" Millie added.

"Admiral Harding," Jacinta offered.

"Jacinta!" the group sighed.

"Well, I was just saying."

"Are you sure it's not Dr. Lush?" Millie asked. "I mean, after everything with that case."

"What case?" Sep asked.

Millie hurriedly blurted the entire tale of Neville and his case and the doctor's identical one.

"Sorry, Neville," she apologized. "They were going to find out sooner or later."

Neville shrugged his shoulders. "It's okay."

"So you're a stowaway?" Jacinta gasped. "Oh, that's so romantic."

The children chortled with laughter.

Alice-Miranda was thinking out loud. "If they are after jewels, then surely they won't leave the ship without the Fabergé eggs in the drawing room. It's just next door. I mean, they're probably more valuable than all of the other gems put together. And who would have had access to all the rooms on the ship? I mean, your man Henderson, we know that he could get into your room, Neville, so he could well have taken that laundry bag, but it's likely someone more senior. Everyone seems so lovely and kind. I can't imagine who it might be. . . ."

A key jiggled in the lock and the library door swung open. The children leapt into the air.

"Quiet, it's just me," Dr. Lush commanded as he walked into the room. "I thought you might be here."

Alice-Miranda spoke first. "Hello, Dr. Lush. Do you know what's going on?"

"It's chaos and—well, no, not really. But I had to get out of that ballroom. You should have heard them all, arguing worse than children."

"I think someone should go and see if the eggs are still in the cabinet next door," Alice-Miranda suggested.

Lucas and Sep offered immediately.

"But what if you catch them in the act? Then what will you do?" Jacinta asked.

Her face crumpled and she started to cry. "I can't believe this sort of thing is happening again."

"Again?" Sep and Neville looked at each other.

"Jacinta, don't be silly." Alice-Miranda shot her a steely look.

"I'll come with you," Dr. Lush volunteered. "I used to be in the Russian navy. I think I could still put up a half-decent fight."

"Wait, there was one thing," Alice-Miranda called. "All those notes, they looked as if they were written on the exact same size squares of paper. Not notepaper and not quite letter-sized. I saw one of the crew cutting up some paper when I was on the bridge the day we arrived. Then I saw him again yesterday in the corridor with a clipboard and lots of little squares of paper pinned under the clasp. We chatted for a moment. That's why I noticed the paper."

"Who was it?" Lush demanded.

"I think . . . yes, it must be. First Officer Prendergast," Alice-Miranda blurted.

"Oh my," Lush murmured. "He came and helped me do inventory yesterday, and at first he was all gushy, bombarding me with loads of questions, but when I asked if he could keep quiet for a while it was as if he turned into another person altogether. It was very peculiar."

Jacinta stood up. "Well, let's see if those eggs are still there." She opened the door to the adjacent drawing room and promptly screamed.

"Hello there, young lady," a voice drifted from the other room. Jacinta shrieked again. A hand reached in and grabbed her, pulling her through the doorway and out of sight.

"Tie her up and gag her. I can't stand the noise," the voice instructed.

"Why are you doing this?" a second voice quavered.

"Shut up, Henderson, you little do-gooder. First you beg me not to tell the admiral that I found the royal standard you'd stolen and hidden in your locker, and now you want to let the sniveling brat go!"

"But I didn't steal the standard," the man protested.

"Of course you didn't. But how else was I going to get you to do all those special little errands for me? I never realized how attached some people are to their professions."

"I didn't mind helping you with the laundry, but now you've gone too far. I don't tie up little girls."

"Well, you weren't moving laundry either, you imbecile. What did you think was in those sacks? Dirty socks?"

The other man sniffed. "How was I to know what you were up to?"

"Well, you weren't to know, were you? But you've been awfully helpful. And I'm sure that you're going to make very tasty fish food. Now get in there and take that little minx with you."

Jacinta and Henderson entered the library. First Officer Whitley Prendergast strode into the room and stood directly behind the pair.

"Jacinta!" Alice-Miranda rushed toward her friend.

"Stop right there!" Prendergast commanded.

Alice-Miranda stood her ground. "You've got no right."

"No, but I've got this little baby and I'm certainly

not afraid to use it." Prendergast produced a shiny black handgun from inside his coat.

Alice-Miranda stopped.

Henderson looked at Neville. *I'm sorry,* he mouthed to his small charge.

"All of you, sit down. Henderson, tie them up, and do it properly." Prendergast threw his unwitting assistant a handful of plastic-bag ties.

Millie looked at the ties and then at Sep. The pair exchanged puzzled glances.

"Haven't you heard, kids? They're quite the latest thing in tie-up technology." Prendergast flashed a terrifying grin.

"And don't get any ideas about great escapes, Lush. It's quite my good fortune that you're here with the children. This way you won't be able to embark on any heroic rescue missions."

"What are you talking about?" Lush demanded.

"My dear, dear doctor." Prendergast leered like a shark in a school of baitfish. "You don't think I'd have been foolish enough not to have some additional diversions sorted? You know the medication you took up to Her Majesty this afternoon? The one to keep her allergies at bay? Poor woman, always coming out in those hideous welts, struggling to breathe.

Well, I switched the tablets this afternoon. And so, in about ten minutes' time, when her batty old lady-in-waiting, Mrs. Marmalade, hands her the pills, as she does every day like clockwork, I'm afraid the old girl won't be doing anything very helpful about those allergies. And you, my dear man, will have killed the Queen. No one will care a zot about what happened to the loot."

"What have you done, you monster?" Lush roared. He wriggled in his seat, rocking the chair wildly on its back legs.

"Don't you want to know what will kill our beloved monarch? Well, we all know she's allergic to crustaceans, don't we? I believe there's a wonderful new joint remedy on the market—made from, well, what do you know, crustaceans. Imagine that? A perfectly harmless little tablet . . . for most."

The children could hardly believe what they were hearing. Prendergast *was* a monster.

"So settle down. All of you," Prendergast demanded.

"What are you going to do with Jacinta?" Millie demanded.

"Keep your hair on, little one. She's just some extra security. We'll give her back. But I hope she's a strong swimmer."

"You brute." Millie's face looked as if her freckles had caught alight.

"Mr. Prendergast," Alice-Miranda began. "I'm sure that you don't really want to do any of this, do you?"

"Of course I do. Do you think this is my first job? Hardly."

"But you've been a reliable member of this crew for years now. Everyone thinks you're a good fellow," said Dr. Lush. "The admiral treats you like a son."

"Yes, well, that was the old Whitley, you see."

Dr. Lush was trying to work out whether Prendergast was pure evil or if he was suffering some sort of multiple personality disorder.

"Are you unwell, Mr. Prendergast?" Alice-Miranda soothed. "Because I'm sure that we can get you the right help and you'll be better in no time."

"Save it, Pollyanna," Prendergast sneered. "Anyway, must fly. Boat to launch, plane to catch, money to spend, life to live and all that. And by the way, my twin brother, Whitley Prendergast, won't be returning to his old post anytime soon."

Lush drew in a sharp breath. "What do you mean, your twin brother?"

The children looked at each other. "If you're not Whitley, then who are you?" Alice-Miranda asked.

"Arthur. Arthur Prendergast, at your service. Now,

out!" Prendergast motioned at Henderson. "And take her with you."

The trio slipped through the door into the drawing room. The sound of Jacinta's muffled screams felt like a knife twisting in Alice-Miranda's stomach.

"What will he do with her and poor Mr. Henderson?" Neville gasped.

"I'm sure Jacinta will be fine," said Alice-Miranda firmly. "She's very fit and much tougher than she looks. And Mr. Henderson's a strong man. We just have to hope he has an opportunity to get away." But Alice-Miranda was worried. It seemed that Arthur Prendergast was not a man to be underestimated.

"Where is everyone?" Lucas frowned. "I would have thought someone would be down to look for us by now."

The ship had become eerily quiet in the past few minutes. Alice-Miranda had a very bad feeling.

"Come on, we've got to get out of here." She wriggled around in her seat. "Are there any scissors in here?"

Dr. Lush came to the rescue. "Yes, there's a cupboard over there behind the couch and a first-aid kit in there too."

Lucas stood up, and although he was still tied to his chair, he managed to walk and hop over to the cupboard and pry open the door with his foot. In another minute he'd located the scissors and freed himself and everyone else in the room.

"Dr. Lush, you must get to Aunty Gee before she takes that pill," Alice-Miranda instructed.

"I bet they're heading for the dock at the rear of the ship," Sep spoke.

"The boats—that's how he's planning to get the jewels off the ship," Lucas added.

"Come on, we know how to get there." Alice-Miranda led the charge. "We can't let them take Jacinta."

"What about the jewels?" Sep called.

"Who cares about the jewels? But if anything happens to Jacinta I'll never forgive myself," Alice-Miranda called back over her shoulder.

Chapter 42

Nicholas Lush soon realized why no one else had left the ballroom to look for the children. Prendergast and his unwitting accomplice had barricaded the doors. It sounded like an angry mob on the other side. Lush could only hope that in the chaos, Mrs. Marmalade had forgotten all about the Queen's medication.

It seemed he arrived just in time. Lush threw open the doors as Aunty Gee raised a glass to her lips. "Noooooo!" he called as he raced across the room and launched himself at her over the table.

"For heaven's sake, man, what are you doing?" Queen Georgiana yelled as the doctor knocked the glass from her hand and showered her with water. "Are you trying to kill me?"

"Medication," Nicholas gasped. "Poison. *They* were going to kill you."

Queen Georgiana looked as if she'd been stung. "Oh dear me. I suppose I should say thank you, then."

Alice-Miranda's immediate family gathered around Lush as he picked himself up from the floor.

"Have you seen the children?" Hugh Kennington-Jones demanded.

"Yes, they've gone after them. Prendergast has the blond girl. And Henderson's with him, but I don't think he's there by choice." Lush was still gasping for air after his heroics.

"Jacinta?" Ambrosia Headlington-Bear had been sitting with Mrs. Oliver, who was trying to console the silly woman about her missing necklace. "Did you say they have my Jacinta?"

"Yes," Lush replied.

"Noooo!" Ambrosia wailed. She felt like she couldn't breathe. "My baby, please don't let them hurt my little girl." Fat, frightened tears erupted from her eyes and streamed down her blotchy face.

"There's no time to lose," Lawrence muttered. "Come on, Hugh. Lush, get over here. You need to show us where they've gone."

Chapter 43

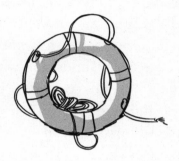

"There they are!" Alice-Miranda whispered as she caught sight of Prendergast attempting to lower the small vessel into the water. "We've got to stop him."

The children scurried down the steps as quietly as they could. Alice-Miranda spied a pile of laundry bags sitting on the dock.

"I've got a plan," she said. "We need to get to those bags before they load them."

"But how?" asked Lucas.

Henderson and Prendergast were standing near a switchboard arguing.

"Hurry up. We need to get off this tub," Prendergast snapped.

"I'm doing my best." Henderson sniffed.

"I thought you said that you'd trained on every inch of this ship," Prendergast hissed.

Henderson's voice quavered. "Well, almost."

Jacinta was standing near the laundry bags whimpering—she was bound and gagged and tied to a long piece of rope that Henderson was hanging on to.

"Shut up, you!" Prendergast was losing any shred of patience he had left. He pulled out his gun and pointed it at Henderson.

"Get that boat in the water!" he roared. "NOW!"

Henderson hit a yellow button on the control panel. The small powerboat hanging from its mechanical arm shot up toward the top of the rigging.

"What are you doing, man? Give it to me." Prendergast elbowed the steward out of the way. He reached out with his spindly fingers. "Eeny, meeny, miny, mo." He hit another button and the mechanical arm swung out over the sea in preparation to lower the boat. "See, it wasn't that hard, now, was it?" he asked with a smirk.

"Look," Neville whispered. "I think that's another control panel over there. It looks the same."

"Can you operate it, Neville?" Alice-Miranda looked hopeful.

"I—I—I don't know. I can try." Neville studied the buttons and wondered if they would work when the other panel was already in use. "Here goes." He hit a green button and the boom that had swung out over the water began to swing back toward the ship.

"What the . . ." Prendergast was seething. He pushed another button and the arm swung back out over the sea.

Neville pressed his button and the boom swung back again. He pressed another button and the second boat, which the children had been out on that morning, swung over the water. Prendergast fiddled with the control panel below and the boat swung back again. It was like an aerial boat ballet. Prendergast was engrossed in trying to figure out the control panel lest both boats come crashing down. The children were crouched down out of sight behind some large machinery. As the game continued, Sep and Lucas raced down the short flight of stairs onto the lower deck. The whir of the pulley system and hum of the engine room was enough to drown out the sound of them throwing the laundry sacks back up to Millie and Alice-Miranda. Jacinta had seen her friends and was staring at them with frightened eyes. Alice-Miranda held her finger to her lips, begging her to stay quiet.

Prendergast looked as if he was set to explode.

"Get in the water, you stupid boat!" he roared. At that very moment, Neville pressed a big red button and the ropes unraveled at great speed, depositing the smaller vessel into the sea with a loud crash and sending the jet boat hurtling down alongside it.

"Get the sacks!" Prendergast yelled at Henderson as he leapt down into the boat. As he did, his gun flew out of his right hand and disappeared into the sea. "Curses!" Prendergast looked over the side, but the weapon was well and truly gone. He turned his attention to getting the engine started. "Hurry up with those sacks," he growled.

Henderson turned around and gasped. "They're gone!"

"What do you mean, they're gone?" Prendergast was clearly not much of a sailor and was having a very difficult time keeping the little boat close to the ship, particularly as the larger one was crashing against it.

The two men stood arguing.

"Is this what you're looking for?" Alice-Miranda

stood up from her hiding spot. She held one of the laundry bags aloft. "I've got a deal for you, Mr. Prendergast. You give us Jacinta and Mr. Henderson and I'll give you your bags."

"This is not a game, princess," he snarled. "I don't care if your little friend ends up as bait."

Alice-Miranda stood her ground. "I'm not playing games either, Mr. Prendergast. You give us Jacinta and Mr. Henderson and I'll give you your loot. But you'd better decide soon. I'm sure the admiral and the rest of the crew are on their way down here right now."

"I have a gun, you foolish child!" he yelled.

"No, you don't," Neville called back. "I saw it fall in the water. You were looking for it."

Prendergast's face was the color of overripe tomatoes. He indicated to Henderson to let Jacinta go, but Henderson had already untied her. "Now give me those bags!" Prendergast screamed.

True to Alice-Miranda's word, Lucas and Sep threw the laundry bags down one after the other to Henderson, who promptly hurled them onto the boat.

"Get in!" Prendergast screamed at Henderson.

"No! You're a lunatic."

"Suit yourself." Prendergast engaged the gears and

the outboard sputtered to life. And just like that, he disappeared into the murky night.

Alice-Miranda tore the gag from Jacinta's mouth.

"Thank you," Jacinta blubbered. "You saved my life."

"No," Alice-Miranda replied. "You can thank Neville. He distracted them so we could get the laundry bags."

"I hope someone finds him," Neville spoke.

"I'm so sorry." Henderson was shaking. "Please believe me. I didn't know what I was doing. Prendergast said that if I didn't help him with some jobs here and there, he'd tell the admiral that the royal standard was in my locker. He said that I would be court-martialed and thrown off the *Octavia* for good. I love working on board, and I can't think of anything else in the world I'd rather do. So I just looked after his laundry bags. I didn't know . . ."

Neville walked over, reached up and touched the steward on the shoulder.

"It's all right, Mr. Henderson. I believe you," he said.

"Of course we believe you." Alice-Miranda nodded.

"But the rotten brute still got away with all those lovely jewels," Jacinta fumed.

"I don't know about that," Lucas sniggered. Jacinta

spun around to see Lucas and Sep prancing about in diamond tiaras.

"But how?"

"Tool kit." Sep pointed at an empty box. "We swapped the tools for the tiaras."

"He'll be furious," Jacinta giggled.

Chapter 44

Hugh Kennington-Jones and Lawrence Ridley could hardly believe their eyes when they found the children and Henderson in the dock. Admiral Harding had alerted the coast guard, who were on the lookout for Prendergast. He couldn't believe Neville's quick thinking—the lad was a hero. And as for Henderson, the admiral said that it was lucky he was still alive.

Aunty Gee insisted that once the jewels were returned to their rightful owners, the party should recommence—although Vladimir was heard protesting loudly that the food was "no longer fit to serve for

Queen." As it was only nine p.m. there was still time for a small supper and a dance, at least.

Upon sight of her only daughter, Ambrosia Headlington-Bear began to bawl like a baby. She tore across the ballroom and hugged Jacinta as though her very life depended on it.

"I've got your choker, Mummy." Jacinta managed to release herself from her mother's viselike grip.

"Oh, Jacinta, I don't care about that at all. When I heard they'd taken you, I didn't know what to do. I've been the most awful mother," she sobbed.

Jacinta didn't quite know what to do either. She had never seen her mother like this. So she did the first thing that came to mind and agreed with her, then launched into a very solid telling-off for never visiting her at school or taking her on holidays or paying her the slightest bit of attention. But for the first time ever, her mother had no response.

That night the children fell into bed utterly exhausted. At least the wedding could go ahead the next evening. Nothing could spoil it now.

The girls awoke to a perfect morning. Millie pulled back the curtains to reveal a sparkling view of the coastline.

"This is going to be the best day ever." Alice-Miranda leapt from her bed and gave Jacinta a hug before tearing over to the window to give Millie the same.

"Good morning, young ladies," said Winterstone as he appeared at the bedroom door. "I trust you slept well after last night's adventures?"

"Oh yes, Mr. Winterstone. It *was* rather adventurous wasn't it? But everyone's fine now, and today is going to be wonderful." Alice-Miranda charged over to the old man and gave him an unexpected hug.

"Oh goodness, what was that for?" he said, trembling.

"Just because," she whispered. "And I love your new haircut too."

The old man blushed. "Ahem, there's been a delivery for you, miss."

"Oh, how exciting. May I have it, please?" Alice-Miranda asked.

"I'm afraid you're going to have to collect this one in person. From Admiral Harding's study."

"That sounds intriguing."

Alice-Miranda rushed to the bathroom and washed her face. By the time she returned to the bedroom, Winterstone had already laid out her clothes for the day, along with Jacinta's and Millie's.

"Thank you, Mr. Winterstone," the tiny child called to the steward, who was busying himself pouring juice in the sitting room. He allowed himself the pleasure of a small smile.

Alice-Miranda dressed and headed off to see the admiral. She wondered what on earth could have arrived that had to be delivered to his study all the way up on the bridge. Alice-Miranda knocked loudly before being summoned inside.

"Sloane!" she gasped. "How wonderful to see you!"

Neville Nordstrom was standing beside Sloane Sykes and two men she didn't recognize. From the shock of snowy hair and caterpillar eyebrows, she guessed that the shorter one was Neville's father, and the taller man looked rather like Sloane. Aunty Gee was seated beside Admiral Harding, with Dalton hovering close behind. Next to the admiral, Alice-Miranda was surprised to see a familiar face, although she'd never met the man before.

"Hello, everyone." Alice-Miranda looked around. She offered her hand to the short man with the fair hair. "My name's Alice-Miranda Highton-Smith-Kennington-Jones."

"Lenny Nordstrom." The man nodded and took her hand into his.

The taller man shook her hand as well. "Smedley Sykes."

"Oh, how lovely to finally meet you, Mr. Sykes. I've heard so much about you from Sep!" she exclaimed. The man grinned.

Alice-Miranda walked over and shook the final man's hand. "Hello, President Grayson. It's an honor to meet you and a wonderful surprise. I hadn't expected to see you today. Are you staying for the wedding?"

The handsome man with the chiseled jaw smiled broadly. "It's lovely to meet you too, miss, and yes, Her Majesty has suggested we stay for the night. And you know, it's pretty hard to say no to her," he drawled in his delicious Southern twang.

"Good morning, Aunty Gee," Alice-Miranda greeted the monarch.

Queen Georgiana gathered the tiny child into a bear hug.

"I believe you've got quite a tale to tell, young lady," Admiral Harding said seriously.

"Oh, Admiral, I am sorry. I didn't mean to keep Neville a secret. It's just that things got so very complicated these past couple of days and . . ."

Admiral Harding held up his hand to stop her babbling. "Alice-Miranda, I'm sure that you will regale us with the full tale later. But thanks to your harboring young Neville with the very dirty shoes, and writing that letter—golly, I am impressed by how this royal mail system works—you've helped capture Prendergast and saved Her Majesty's life."

"But how?" Alice-Miranda gasped. "We watched him get away last night."

"Well," Sloane began. "It all started yesterday afternoon when I took your letter around to Neville's parents. I was showing them what you'd written to me when there was another visitor—a rather unexpected one." She pointed at President Grayson. "President Grayson was so surprised about what you said that he organized straight away for us to come and make sure that Neville was all right."

"But how did you find us so quickly?" Alice-Miranda asked.

"Well, for a start, you wrote the letters on the paper from the *Octavia*," Sloane began.

"I know. I did that on purpose, I'm afraid." Alice-Miranda flicked an apologetic smile at Neville. "I'd promised Neville that I wouldn't tell his parents where we were, but I rather hoped you'd pick up on that clue."

"And President Grayson *is* the President of the United States," Sloane replied. "He has access to quite a few resources."

"Oh, of course he does. You should be a detective, Sloane."

"Thank you. Anyway, let me get back to the story." She was clearly reveling in this. "On the way out, we saw a boat bobbing about in the waves. Smoke was pouring from the engine, and there was a man on board cursing madly. A message had come through from Interpol to be on the lookout for him. President Grayson's security men picked him up. And now we're here," Sloane finished.

"But what about the butterflies?" Alice-Miranda asked.

"That's another story. And I'm starving. Do you think we could talk about it over some breakfast?" Sloane asked.

"Oh yes, please." Alice-Miranda smiled. "Millie and Jacinta and the boys will be so surprised to see you all."

Alice-Miranda raced over and gave Sloane a tight hug. She hugged Neville too.

Chapter 45

That evening, Aunt Charlotte and Uncle Lawrence were married under a moonlit sky on the Royal Deck. Alice-Miranda was an adorable flower girl in her pale pink organza dress, carrying a bouquet of matching peonies. Charlotte was breathtaking in a stunning white gown, with a lace bodice and full silk skirt, and Lawrence Ridley lived up to his status as the most handsome movie star on the planet.

At the reception, the ballroom sparkled under thousands of fairy lights and the reflection of hundreds of jewels. It seemed that most of the female guests had taken their style tips from Lady Sarah and were wearing every piece of jewelry they owned.

"Aren't they perfect together?" Alice-Miranda said as she watched the happy couple making their way onto the dance floor.

"Absolutely, cuz," Lucas replied as he smiled at his father and new stepmother.

As members of the wedding party, Lucas and Alice-Miranda were seated next to each other at the head table, but tonight the rest of the children were sitting with their parents.

Ambrosia Headlington-Bear was trying to make up for lost time with Jacinta.

"I'll come to school and take you out during the term, and I might even rent a cottage nearby and then I can spend some time with you during the week too."

Jacinta frowned. "Mummy, please don't overdo it. We need to take things slowly, and remember that most days I'm training. I'd much rather you come and visit me a couple of times than promise me the world and deliver nothing. And I don't need you getting in my way at school. I've done fine by myself for this long, and I don't want you turning into one of those dreadful pushy stage mothers. That would be even worse."

Ambrosia swallowed hard. She wasn't used to being told what to do and was about to respond when something made her stop.

"Of course, darling," she replied.

Then Jacinta did something completely unexpected. She turned around and hugged her mother tightly. Ambrosia Headlington-Bear didn't know what to do. Her arms hovered in the air for a few uncomfortable seconds before she reached out and hugged her daughter right back.

Hugh and Cecelia were standing together with the admiral and Aunty Gee. Dalton was loitering close to Her Majesty. She stepped aside and motioned for him to join her.

"Well, Dalton, this is another fine mess you knew nothing about," she whispered. "Why don't you go and keep Mrs. Marmalade company? I think she needs a dance partner."

"But, ma'am, I don't think I should," Dalton objected.

"Of course you don't, but consider this your punishment. You've gotten off very lightly." Queen Georgiana arched an eyebrow and flicked her hand.

She watched as he grumbled his way across the room to where Mrs. Marmalade was standing on the edge of the dance floor.

"They've located Whitley Prendergast, thank heavens," the admiral advised as Her Majesty rejoined the group. "Apparently his twin brother, Arthur, had recently been released from prison, having served ten years for armed robbery. Whitley was on shore leave two weeks ago, and when Arthur came to call on him, the poor unsuspecting lad gave his brother a place to stay and said that he'd help him find a job."

"Yes, well, I think Arthur helped himself, didn't he?" Hugh added.

"So where has Whitley been all this time?" Aunty Gee inquired.

"The police found him tied up in the basement of his house, almost starved to death and delirious with worry," the admiral replied.

"Oh, poor man." Aunty Gee clasped her hands together.

"I was wondering how Arthur seemed to know everything about the ship. But of course he'd had a full week on board before you arrived for the wedding party. I should have known, though, when he offered to help Lush with that inventory of the medical supplies. Whitley is so dedicated to his role on the bridge he hardly leaves the room when we're at sea. And here I was being taken for a ride, just thinking that it was good for the lad to assist in other areas. Who'd have thought twins could be so incredibly alike and yet so horribly different?"

"So is Arthur responsible for those thefts of Russian jewels as well?" Hugh furrowed his brow.

"No, I think he just saw the *Octavia* providing his retirement fund. I called Inspector Gerard this morning to see whether any of this made sense to him, but he said they have a strong lead with the Russian jewels—they're after some lunatic who thinks he's Alexei Romanov, the murdered son of the last Russian tsar. Gerard said they almost had him last week but he's disappeared again. So, no, Arthur's not mad, just a nasty piece of work," the admiral concluded.

"Oh well, thank heavens everyone's safe," said Aunty Gee. "And this is a lovely wedding."

"Thanks to you, Aunty Gee." Cecelia smiled at her godmother.

On the other side of the room, Sloane and Sep Sykes were sitting together with their father, Smedley, and Neville and his father, Leonard.

"Mummy would have loved all this," Sloane said with a smirk.

"Yes, I think you're right there," her father said. "Perhaps we won't tell her."

"Dad?" Sep shook his head. "Where does she think you are? She must be worried sick."

"Well, I told her that your sister and I had some

urgent business to attend to and we'd be back some-time after Friday."

"Poor Mum." Sep folded his arms in front of him.

"Well, I called my wife, Sylvia, and sent her around to see your September," Leonard Nordstrom explained. "I suggested that they might like a day at the spa—my treat."

"Good plan," Smedley Sykes agreed. "Might go some way to getting me off the hook."

"I hardly think so, Dad," Sloane scoffed. "Mum was whining about not being invited to the wedding and how it was so unfair that Sep got to go. I think you'll be buying her flowers every week for the rest of your life."

Smedley Sykes was lost in his thoughts. He'd spent long enough with September to know that she could hold a grudge. Flowers every week would be getting off very lightly, as far as he was concerned.

Millie was sitting at an adjacent table with her parents and fiddling with her camera.

"I think you've found your calling," her father laughed.

"A photographer?" Millie asked.

"No, a private investigator." He grinned. "Or you could be one of those dreaded paparazzo."

"Very funny, Dad," Millie replied.

"You'll have to check back through all your photographs to see if you don't have any suspicious activity going on in the background," her grandfather laughed.

"I'd like to take a photograph of my family, if I may." Millie urged her parents, grandfather and Mrs. Oliver closer together. She set the timer on the camera, placed it on the table and raced around to sit on her father's lap just as the flash went off.

"How do we look?" her grandfather asked.

Millie reviewed the picture and burst out laughing. "Grandpa! You weren't supposed to be kissing Mrs. Oliver! We have to take another one."

Over in the corner of the room, Vladimir had emerged from the kitchen to survey his feast.

Nicholas Lush was standing nearby and walked over to say hello. "Your food is wonderful," the doctor congratulated him.

"Yes, food is good," Vlad replied. "So, your mother, she was Maria Bella Lushkov?"

"Yes." Dr. Lush nodded. "How did you know?"

"The little one, Alice-Miranda, she bring me the inscription. I translate for her," Vlad replied. "She clever child. I like her."

"Yes," Nicholas agreed.

"And your mother, I love her. She best singer in the world to me," Vlad announced.

"Thank you, Vladimir. Thank you very much." Nicholas Lush reached out and shook the chef's hand.

Sitting among the band members, Alex glanced up and gave the pair a wave.

Back at the Sykeses' table, Smedley was still worrying about how he might appease his wife and was listening to a range of suggestions from the children and Lenny.

"Excuse me, Mr. Nordstrom, may I borrow your son for a moment?" President Grayson interrupted.

"Of course, Your Presidency, I mean, Your Highness, I mean Mr. President." Lenny Nordstrom fumbled his words.

"Please just call me Gatsby." The president slapped Lenny playfully on the back.

"Of course." Lenny's ears turned bright red.

President Grayson led Neville to the corner of the room, where there were a couple of armchairs.

"Please sit," the president directed. "I'm sorry about what happened, son, with us talking on the Internet. It's just that you were too clever and I wasn't."

"What do you mean?" Neville's forehead wrinkled.

"Well, you worked out who I was, and so the Secret Service and the CIA and the FBI and Homeland Security and all those people who have to protect me decided that you were a threat. And that's why I couldn't talk to you anymore. But you'd told me enough, and so I wanted to see for myself. I had to come find you. You're a smart boy, Neville, and we're gonna save those butterflies and we're gonna make sure that habitat is protected forever."

Neville grinned. "Thank you, Mr. President."

Over on the dance floor, Alice-Miranda and Lucas had been taking a twirl, then decided to have a break. Lucas went to get some drinks when Alice-Miranda spied Neville and the president.

"Oh, hello, Neville, Mr. President."

"Hello there, little lady," said the president. "Come join us."

"I didn't mean to intrude," Alice-Miranda replied.

"That's quite all right. Young Neville here was just about to tell me exactly how he discovered that Euchloe Bazae."

"He has the most amazing photographs. You've got to see them."

Neville blushed. "Perhaps we could have breakfast together tomorrow, Mr. President," Neville suggested. "I can show you everything then."

"Well, that sounds perfect, young man, just perfect." President Grayson stood up. "I think I might see if your Aunty Gee fancies a spin around that dance floor."

Alice-Miranda sat down in the armchair opposite Neville.

"Thank you," the boy said, looking at her. His ink-blue eyes sparkled and he grinned widely.

"What for?" Alice-Miranda asked.

"For everything," Neville replied.

Alice-Miranda smiled. "Would you like to?" She glanced toward the dance floor, which was packed with guests.

Neville nodded.

"Okay, but Granny Bert's looking very dangerous out there with that stick—consider yourself officially warned."

Neville took Alice-Miranda's hand and led her into the crowd. Millie and Jacinta, Sloane, Sep and Lucas soon joined them, dancing and twirling and laughing. Millie snapped away, taking photographs of everyone.

"You know," Alice-Miranda said beaming, "this really *is* the best day ever."

And just in case you're wondering . . .

Arthur Prendergast returned to prison for a very long time, convicted of armed robbery, kidnapping and attempted murder of the Queen—but he wouldn't own up to bringing the prawns on board. His brother Whitley spent a few days in the hospital recovering from his ordeal and returned to work to a rousing welcome. Henderson was given a stern talking-to from the admiral but was relieved to keep his job.

Upon reaching their destination in Venice, Dr. Lush and Alex invited Alice-Miranda to go ashore with them. The tiny child stood in silence on the Rialto Bridge over the Grand Canal as the two men scattered their beloved mother, Maria Bella, to the wind, just as she had wanted.

Mr. Winterstone took Alice-Miranda's advice and decided that he would try to inject some fun into his life. The first thing he did was take a spin on the new jet boat with Her Majesty, Granny Valentina and a very attentive Dalton.

Sloane Sykes turned over a new leaf. She promised to write to Alice-Miranda and secretly hoped she might convince her father to allow her to go back to Winchesterfield-Downsfordvale.

Neville had been wrong about the butterfly in the frame. It hadn't belonged to his grandfather at all. It was his father's. It seemed Leonard loved butterflies as much as the president.

Neville Nordstrom and President Grayson became firm friends. With their shared love of butterflies, together they saved the Euchloe Bazae and its habitat. The land's owner, Smedley Sykes, didn't take too much convincing to find a new location for his next villa project. As he saw it, there were plenty of good sites in Spain, and the new owner had paid him a handsome return on his investment. The property was turned over to the local government under the provision that it remain open parkland forever. Neville's discovery was written up in *Scientific Scientist* and he was hailed as a hero. His parents couldn't have been more proud.

Cast of Characters

{327}

Mrs. Shillingsworth	Head housekeeper
Granny Bert (Albertine Rumble)	Former housekeeper, lives on the property in Rose Cottage
Daisy Rumble	Granddaughter of Granny Bert—lives with her in Rose Cottage and works as a maid at Highton Hall
Harold Greening	Gardener
Maggie Greening	Harold's wife

FRIENDS AND FAMILY OF THE HIGHTON-SMITH-KENNINGTON-JONES FAMILY

Aunty Gee	Granny Highton-Smith's best friend and Cecelia's godmother (among other things!)
Lady Sarah Adams	Cecelia and Charlotte's cousin
Lord Robert Adams	Lady Sarah's husband
Annie Adams	Eldest daughter of Sarah and Robert
Poppy Adams	Youngest daughter of Sarah and Robert
Millicent Jane McLoughlin-McTavish-McNoughton-McGill	Alice-Miranda's best friend and roommate
Jacinta Headlington-Bear	Talented gymnast, school's former second-best tantrum-thrower and a friend

Lucas Nixon	Lawrence Ridley's son and soon to be Alice-Miranda's cousin
Septimus Sykes	Lucas's best friend and brother of Sloane
Sloane Sykes	Ex-student at Winchesterfield-Downsfordvale

CREW OF THE *OCTAVIA*

Admiral Teddy Harding	Commander
Whitley Prendergast	First officer
Henderson	Steward
Winterstone	Steward
Dr. Nicholas Lush	Ship's doctor
Alexander Lushkov	Band member
Vladimir	Chef

OTHERS

September Sykes	Mother of Sloane and Septimus
Smedley Sykes	Father of Sloane and Septimus
Neville Nordstrom	Young lad
Leonard and Sylvia Nordstrom	Neville's parents
Dalton	Personal bodyguard to Aunty Gee
Mrs. Marmalade	Lady-in-waiting

About the Author

Jacqueline Harvey has spent her working life teaching in girls' boarding schools. She's never cruised aboard the *Octavia,* but she has come across quite a few girls who remind her a little of Alice-Miranda.

Jacqueline has published fifteen novels for young readers in her native Australia. Her first picture book, *The Sound of the Sea,* was named a Children's Book Council of Australia Honor Book. She is currently working on Alice-Miranda's next adventure.

For more about Jacqueline and Alice-Miranda, visit:

alice-miranda.com

and

jacquelineharvey.com.au